Bulletface 2:

The Bang Bang Theory

By:

Rio

Dedication

This book is dedicated to the memory of Barry "Biggs" Williams.

Prologue

Thursday, May 15, 2014

Pint-sized *Prometh with Codeine* bottles littered the table, some empty, some full, some standing upright while others lay flat on the glass like wounded soldiers. A Ziploc bag containing close to a pound of Kush was also present, as well as several 50-count boxes of White Owl cigarillos, five 32-ounce bottles of Sprite, and an assortment of iPhone5 smartphones that belonged to the five rap artists who were seated on the L-shaped, black leather sofa. Each of them was holding a Glock with a 30-round clip and a double-stacked Styrofoam cup full of Lean.

Bulletface was one of them.

The other four were Young Meach, P.A.T., Will Scrill, and Gibs, a team of exceptional young rappers and even more exceptional dope boys. Meach was from Blake "Bulletface" King's home town of Michigan City, Indiana. The others were Vice Lords from Gary, Indiana. Blake had given each of them $2 million in drug money on top of their $5 million bonus for signing with his record label. Now they were all in his glossy black Newell tour bus leaving an MBM concert at the United Center that had just netted Blake a cool $1 million.

"Can't believe I ain't caught that nigga T-Walk yet," Blake said, taking a tight sip of Lean and blowing Kush smoke out of his nose. He briefly rested the Glock on his lap to pass Meach the blunt, and then it was right back in his hand. "He think it's a game, bruh. Them niggas done shot me twelve times. They killed Lil Mike, Young-D, shot Meach seven times in Miami. It's yellow tape when I see that nigga."

"He can't hide forever," Meach said.

Will Scrill added, "We at war in the G, too. It's gon' be a hot summer for everybody this year."

Blake nodded thoughtfully. He wore Louis Vuitton from head to toe, and the Le Vian diamonds on his neck, wrists, and pinkies were worth more than five million dollars. He was the self-proclaimed king of the Midwest, the king of the dope game and, according to the latest Forbes list, the king of Hip-Hop. Often compared to Cash Money's CEO, Birdman, Bulletface now had an official billion-dollar net worth, a first for the Hip-Hop community. He also had an unlimited reach into the billions upon billions that his beautiful black and Mexican girlfriend had at her disposal.

He had two white iPhone5s stacked on the table. One of them lit up with a text message from Alexus.

"Are you gonna come in here and fuck me? I'm in here naked and you're out there smoking with your friends, lol. Lame."

"Got me fucked up," he texted back.

Half a second later, he excused himself from the gang with a quickly voiced, "Be back."

"Haaaa," Meach laughed. "Queen-A call and that nigga goes running. Can't knock you for dat, bruh."

"Aw, you know I'm on baby," Blake shouted over his shoulder.

He was already at the bedroom door. There were three bedrooms on the tour bus; one for him, one for Alexus, and one for her bodyguards.

The door was unlocked. He pushed it open and stood in utter amazement at the beautiful Alexus Costilla.

Wearing only a pink wig and a pair of six-inch peep-toe Louboutin heels, she was standing at the dresser mirror with her long black hair tied back in a ponytail, thumbing through Instagram on her iPhone5. She was as thick as Tahiry in the rear, and her flawless reddish-brown face, lightly veiled in make-up, drew Bulletface in like a moth to a flame. Her pretty green eyes were studying the wealthy young gangsta rapper in the reflection of the mirror. She had her tongue sticking halfway out between her teeth, the tip of it seductively tracing her upper lip.

"Mind if I turn into Pinky the Pornstar for an hour or two?" Alexus said, turning and sashaying over to where Bulletface stood at the door.

"I was wondering what the pink hair was about," Bulletface replied.

"What do you mean? I'm pinky. My hair is always pink."

"Yeah, a'ight." A narrow grin revealed the platinum and diamonds on Bulletface's teeth.

Alexus squatted before him and had his pants and underwear pulled down to his knees a moment later. Taking his heavy log of a penis in both hands, she squeezed and twisted at its base and gave its head a gentle kiss.

Then her head became a blur.

She began slurping his long black pole in and out of her mouth, stroking it with one hand while cradling his scrotum in the other. Her throat made squishy wet noises as she sucked in as much of his foot-long as she possibly could.

Bulletface put his Glock in the shoulder-holster under his left arm and leaned back on the door, smiling contentedly. His tour bus was en route to the MBM after-party at Adrianna's, a popular nightclub in Markham, Illinois where all of the top rap artists, mobsters, and dope boys went to party and mingle.

The pink-colored tour bus that was trailing behind Bulletface's belonged to Mocha, his platinum-selling R&B artist. The three white Tahoes that were following the pink Newell coach were full of more armed bodyguards.

Though he would never admit it, Bulletface was more than a little worried about the club appearance. A few weeks prior, He'd released a song featuring Migos, the Atlanta rap group that Chief Keef was currently at odds with. Keef had voiced his thoughts on the collaboration via Twitter:

"How u the 'King of the Midwest' and u fuckin' wit niggas dat don't like us?"

A second tweet had read:

"Playin' both side shit dat I'on like! War time spark broad day light!"

Bulletface had not taken the threat lightly, and knowing that Keef's GBE crew was also scheduled to perform tonight at Adrianna's had him feeling uneasy.

Momentarily, Alexus' tightly sucking mouth relieved him of that uneasiness.

He stepped out of his pants and underwear. Then he picked her up and flipped her upside down in a standing sixty-nine. He'd seen the move on a Pinky XXX video. Since Alexus Costilla had suddenly decided to transform herself into Pinky, he figured it best to treat her like the red-boned porn star.

He licked and sucked on her clitoris for a while, and he would have continued tonguing her juicy pussy if the gunfire had not begun.

Fredo had fifty rounds in his AK-47, and Reese had an additional fifty rounds in his Mac-11 when Ballout pulled alongside the Bulletface tour bus in a dark-colored Explorer he'd rented from a crack-head on 64th and Normal.

As Fredo and Reese hung out of the passenger's side windows and opened fire on the tour bus. All Ballout could think about was the two hundred kilograms of coke the GBE squad was getting for the hit on Bulletface. The kilos were coming from a middle-aged Hispanic woman who'd contacted Keef for the deal shortly after hearing of his burgeoning beef with Bulletface.

The woman's name was Sophia.

Chapter 1

Blake fell over sideways, flipping Alexus upright and pulling her down with him in the process. He drew his pistol from its holster and sent a dozen booming rounds in return, scurrying to his left with Alexus because bullets were chopping through the right side of the wall across from them.

His eyes became glued to the darkly-tinted bedroom window, and he saw the gunmen's faces just as they were slipping back into their escaping SUV. Their tires screeched as they made a hasty turn down an alleyway. Alexus' bodyguards were rushing toward the alley with their submachine guns blazing.

Blake got up and dressed hurriedly. He was pulling up his pants when Enrique, Alexus' head of security, burst into the bedroom. There was blood on his face and neck.

"Bastards hit two of my men," Enrique said. "Blake, you're not gonna like it out there."

Blake checked on Alexus to make sure she wasn't hurt; her eyes were agape as she shimmied into a one-shouldered mini-dress, and her hands were trembling.

Then, still gripping the Glock in one strong, veiny, black hand, he walked out to where his MBM team had been seated across from his glassed-in recording booth.

P.A.T. had a palm pressed to his bloodied shoulder.

Young Meach and Scrill were standing over Yellowboy's grounded figure.

Tall and lean, light-complected and dreadlocked like MMG's Gunplay, Yellowboy was stretched out on the floor between the sofa and the blood-covered table.

There was a large hole an inch to the right of his nose.

Chapter 2

"More drone strikes in Mexico as U.S. forces continue their hunt for the elusive Jennifer Costilla. It is believed that she is being aided by the Sinaloa drug cartel, which is why several Sinaloa strongholds have been the target of American drone attacks. The FBI has raised the "Dead or Alive" reward for Jenny Costilla's capture to twenty million dollars, doubling the amount previously offered for Osama bin Laden after the nine-eleven attacks.

"Meanwhile, just hours ago in Chicago, Jennifer Costilla's niece—American billionaire Alexus Costilla—was on a tour bus with rapper Bulletface and other Money Bagz Management recording artists when an SUV pulled up beside them and fired over thirty shots into the tour bus. Two gunmen reportedly opened fire from inside the SUV before speeding away, leaving rapper Yellowboy and two bodyguards dead and another rapper wounded. This incident only adds to the long list of shootings Bulletface has been involved in. A lot of people are asking the question, 'Why does Alexus keep going back to Bulletface?' Behind Gill Gates, Alexus is the richest person in America. What's she doing with a gangster rapper for a boyfriend? Tomorrow night on AC360, I will be live at The Versace Mansion with the Costilla Corporation CEO herself. If you have questions you would like me to ask Alexus Costilla, post them on my Facebook page, or tweet them to—"

Blake hit the power button on the remote and watched the 100-inch flat screen go black. He gritted his teeth cantankerously and toked in a mouthful of loud smoke.

He and Alexus were standing in the living room of a beachfront mansion that boasted curved glass walls, indoor and outdoor swimming pools, a guest house, and an eight-car garage.

Blake was livid, as were the Costilla Cartel bodyguards who now stood in every room on the first floor of the mansion, armed with AR-15 assault rifles.

Following the shooting, Blake and Alexus had spoken briefly with Chicago police officers. Both claimed to have not seen the gunmen. Then their attorney, Britney Bostic, had arrived and gotten them out of there.

Now it was near midnight in the mansion-lined Long Beach neighborhood of Michigan City, Indiana.

Blake was ready to go back to Chicago.

"We are not going back to Chicago," Alexus stated sternly.

"*You* might not be goin' back," Blake retorted through stringently clenched teeth. "I'm most *definitely* goin' back—"

"No, Blake. You can't. Send your shooters, or I'll send mine, but you can't go back yourself. That's what they're expecting from you. I say we wait it out for a few days. Let me do this interview with Anderson Cooper tomorrow. I'll shift all the attention to my aunt Jenny. It's Thursday night now; we'll drop twenty bodies in that rap guy's Englewood neighborhood by Sunday night."

A small grin burgeoned on Blake's dark-brown face. He took a pull from his blunt and looked down at the gold-plated AK-47 in his left hand. It held a golden 100-round drum.

What would Jay-Z do? He thought to himself. Big homie Hove seemed to have it all figured out. Jay was always either at a show, at a multimillion-dollar business deal, or vacationing somewhere with Queen Bey.

"Niggas like Jay-Z and Kanye get to lay up in Paris with their wives," Blake said as his eyes ascended from Alexus' spiked Louboutin heels to the voluminous hips of her white Pucci dress and finally to her seductive green eyes. "Me, I'm here like Gucci Mane and Boosie, like Chief Keef and the old T.I. I'm plugged into the streets. This war shit will be the death of me."

Shaking her head worriedly, Alexus sauntered over to stand in front of Blake. The platinum necklace she wore was full of white diamonds that were as large and round as silver dollars. A bracelet of equally-sized diamonds encircled her wrist. The alluring scent of her perfume was like a piece of heaven.

"Old age will be the death of you," she said, mashing her glossy pink lips against his. "I can't go for anything else. Now let's go to bed."

And with that, she preceded him to their upstairs bedroom.

Chapter 3

"MMMmmm, MMMmmm, MMMmmm…" Alexus' continuous moans grew loud and then quiet incessantly; loud when he sank his lengthy phallus into her, barely audible when he pulled it out. She dug her perfectly manicured fingernails into his back and gazed up at him, mouth and eyes wide, yelping passionately at his every thrust.

"You like it like this?" Blake grinned down at her.

"Oooooh, yeah."

"You sure about that?"

"Yessss, Blake."

He had her knees pinned to the bed beside her shoulders, hammering in and out of her juicy love tunnel. Moonlight shone through the floor-to-ceiling windows, illuminating Alexus' blissful expression. Twice she shook and trembled beneath him in orgasm, making her creamy center even creamier as Blake continued mercilessly.

His smartphone lit up on the bedside table just as his dick began twitching and spurting between her snugly gripping vaginal walls.

Spent, Blake rolled onto his back and panted for a couple of seconds. Cum was still spewing from the bulbous head of his deflating love muscle. It left a white puddle in the middle of hi six-pack.

A moment later, Alexus said, "My legs won't stop shaking." She laid her head on his chest and a euphonious giggle escaped her lips. "You know, every time we're about to fuck, I go in thinking I'm gonna put you to bed, make you tap out, but it always ends with you fucking my brains out. It's because your dick is so damn *huge*."

Blake replied with a short chuckle, rubbing s palm across her lower back as Alexus started planting a trail of kisses from his herculean chest to his half-erect muscle. On her hands and knees, she puckered her lips and slurped up the small pool of semen from his abdomen before picking up his dick and shoving it down her throat.

While Alexus sucked, Blake thought.

He thought about T-Walk, the man who'd become his biggest enemy over the past four years; the man who'd gotten two of his best friends murdered; the man responsible for twelve of the fourteen bullets that had passed through his body; the man who'd disappeared after having two his Gangster Disciples pull a brazen drive-by shooting on him and Alexus in Miami Beach, Florida.

Blake then thought of Chief Keef, the gun-crazy young Black Disciple gang member, and quite possibly the most ruthless gangster rapper of all time. It was Bulletface's first industry beef, and he was almost certain it would conclude with gunshots. That's just how it was with the gangs in Chicago, kill or be killed. It was the only way.

Then there was the foreboding threat from The Costilla Cartel, from Alexus' uncle, Flako, and his son, Pedro. Flako's daughter, Bella, had gotten Blake's parents killed four months ago. Mere hours later, Blake had blown half of Bella's head off with a .50-caliber pistol. He suspected that Flako knew who his daughter's killer was. For one, Flako had not visited Alexus since the day of Bella's murder, and now he only called when it concerned his profit from a drug shipment.

Clearing his mind of the troubling thoughts, Blake gazed down at the foaming saliva that was sliding down his ebony pole as Alexus held the majority of its length in her throat. He was a tad bit sleepy. A part of him wanted to check his smartphone to see who'd sent him the text message that had come through a few minutes prior, but Alexus' well-honed oral skills had him paralyzed.

He tensed suddenly as a fountain of semen tingled up from his scrotum and filled Alexus' mouth with sticky white goo. She kept her lips sealed around the crown of his pulsating phallus, bobbing gently until the gushing flow of cum ceased. Then she threw her head onto the pillow next to his, squinted and scrunched her face as she swallowed, and smiled like an angel.

"All gone," she chirped.

"That's too nasty," Blake retorted.

"How's it nasty? You don't think it's nasty when you skeet your babies all in my pussy, do you?" She folded back the covers—a white silk sheet and blanket set that she'd taken from The Versace Mansion—and slipped her thick legs underneath them. "I am so sad for Yellowboy's family, and those two bodyguards I lost were former Chicago police officers with wives and children. All this killing is getting to me, Blake. They could have taken our lives tonight."

"It's cool," Blake said, joining her under the covers. "We'll just have to get the tour busses bulletproofed like our cars."

"That won't take away the killing."

"*Nothing* will take away the killing. You're a Mexican cartel boss. I'm a rapper, a dope boy, *and* a Vice Lord. Killing comes with the territory.

Look at how the other cartels operate. They chop off heads and boil niggas in drums. When your father was in charge of the cartel, he stayed cuttin' a muhfucka's head off. I do the same shit. Only difference is I use bullets instead of machetes. Don't worry about nothin'. I got us, baby."

Alexus snuggled up against Blake and sighed.

"You know," she said, "I wouldn't mind dying if it happened while we were together. Seeing you face your face before I leave this earth is the best possible ending for me. I'd die smiling."

"Hopefully, that'll be a long time from now." Blake didn't want to talk about death. The Grim Reaper had already taken most of his closest loved ones. Now all he had was Alexus and the kids. The notion of losing either of them was too painful to ponder. "I didn't even tell the kids goodnight," he said, changing the subject.

"They're fine. My mom took them to see that new Godzilla movie, said they enjoyed it. She's pissed about me being on that tour bus."

"She'll be a'ight."

"Don't underestimate my momma. She'll cuss your ass out and then tell God on you."

Grinning, Blake picked up his phone from the bedside table to read the new text message. It was from Will Scrill, and in the text was a Fox 32 News website link. Blake touched it and read the news article's headline:

FIVE DEAD, NINE WOUNDED IN ENGLEWOOD MASS SHOOTING; NO SUSPECTS IN CUSTODY

Blake fell asleep with a smile on his face.

Chapter 4

*I don't wanna get too specific, but nigga I'm a beast
wit' mine
Central, Pacific, or Eastern time
I'm spittin' terrific on beats wit' rhymes
I'll clench me a strap dat'll heat cha spine and hand
Meach the nine
No lie, joe, da streets is mine
This four-five Colt'll heat cha mind up and serve it
like a piece of pie
Then it's over, da end nigga, peace, goodbye
You leakin' now, and shakin' like you tweakin' out
Fuck-nigga, my gun'll spit and leave ya dome all
runny quick
Choppa clip'll leave you underground on
punishment
And you ain't comin' out until you turn into a
mummy
Knock the brains out cha skully, you'll turn into a
dummy
Aim at the left side of ya 'Lac ride, kid
Clap ya left eye, you'll crash like Left Eye did
Flash the Tec-nine, the blast make ya Teflon rip
Stash the weapons and smash on some let's ride
shit...*

     Splitting open a White Owl cigar in the rear
passenger's seat of his ocean-blue Maybach

Landaulet, clad in a dark blue Gucci suit with matching shades and croc-skin shoes, Trintino "T-Walk" Walkson was halfway irritated by the Bulletface verse that was booming from the speakers of his elegant Mercedes convertible. He was listening to one of Lil Wayne's newest gangsta songs that featured Bulletface, a track that was now the #1 rap song in the country.

Bedecked in a fuchsia-colored Gucci dress that embraced every inch of her steatopygic lower half and left the top halves of her melon-sized breasts exposed, Ashley "Thunder" Hunter sat next to T-Walk, studying her dark brown visage in a MAC makeup mirror she'd pulled from her Gucci bag seconds prior.

"I'm not just a pretty face," she said, turning to T-Walk. "I am much more than a cute black woman with a big butt. I'm not defined by the photo shoots for all those urban magazines, or by that stupid MTN reality show. I'm a great black woman from Port Arthur, Texas, a college graduate like my parents, and all I want out of life is—"

"Will you please be quiet and hand me the weed?" T-Walk interrupted.

"You're so rude." Ashley dug into her shoulder bag and snatched out the sandwich bag she'd stuffed an ounce of Kush in before they left their condo six hours earlier.

A lot had happened since then.

T-Walk had first taken Ashley shopping on Chicago's "Magnificent Mile," a strip of high-end stores on Michigan Avenue. He'd spent seventy-five thousand dollars on a pair of yellow pave diamond earrings that matched the 10-carat stone on her engagement ring, and an additional one hundred thousand dollars in hard-earned drug money went to the dresses, bags, and shoes he'd purchased for her at the Gucci store. A spa treatment for the two of them followed, during which time T-Walk had learned of the Bulletface tour bus shooting while scrolling down his Facebook homepage.

Since then, he'd hardly been able to keep his phone from his ear. He'd spoken to just about every upper-echelon mobster in the Midwest—his own GDs to the Vice Lords, Black P. Stones, Black Souls, Black Disciples, and Four Corner Hustles that he often did business with—and every one of them was talking about the Bulletface and Chief Keef rivalry. Black Disciples versus Traveling Vice Lords. OTF versus Dub Life. GBE against MBM. The war was officially under way. Bodies were already dropping.

Bulletface and Chief Keef were the most feared gangster rappers in Hip-Hop, both known for shooting their guns at anyone opposing them. A war between them would undoubtedly end in murder. T-Walk was hoping his archenemy, Bulletface would be the next dead rap artist in Hip-Hop's long list of murder mysteries.

He held the now empty cigar in his open palm and watched Ashley fill it with buds of Kush. His Maybach was cruising down Chicago Avenue, en route to The Visionary Lounge, a swanky nightclub owned by Reesie Cup, one of T-Walk's closest business associates.

"I can't wait for the day when somebody actually kills Bulletface. He's got to be the luckiest nigga I know," T-Walk said, breaking apart Kush buds. "I had my niggas shoot him ten times, then some bitch he was fuckin' shot him twice, then *I* shot him twice. The nigga just won't die."

"He won't live through this beef," Ashley said confidently. "Every nigga who runs with Chief Keef is a shooter. They think about guns while the majority of street niggas worldwide are thinking about dollars. That's why you always hear "Bang Bang' in Keef's songs. He says that shit because he does that shit. Every nigga he's beefed with in Chicago—from JoJo to Fathead to Tooka—they're all dead, all shot to death. Only reason Migos aren't dead is because they don't live here or hang out here, unlike Bulletface who's here almost every day he's not on tour. Trust me, every time they catch Bulletface, they'll be shooting. He doesn't stand a chance."

Nodding his head and smiling thoughtfully, T-Walk sealed the blunt with a swipe of his tongue.

"Bang Bang," he said in a tone that was just as thoughtful as his smile.

He sat back and lit the blunt, then checked the time on his iPhone5 and saw that it was ten minutes past midnight.

T-Walk's night was just beginning.

He dialed a 219 number and put his phone to his ear, casting a quick glance out of the rear window to make sure his rented U-Haul truck was still following close behind. It was there, about four car-lengths back.

"What up, big folks?" Lil Ant answered, sounding enthused as always. Lil Ant was a Gangster Disciple from Gary, Indiana, a cold-hearted killer with a cheerful disposition. He'd been shot by Bulletface a few years ago, and his best friend, Reggie, had died in the same incident.

Lil Ant could not wait to get his gun sights on Bulletface.

"Where you at, G-Ball?" T-Walk asked.

"At my lil sister's party in Hammond. Just heard about that tour bus shootin'. Wish they would've killed that nigga."

"Wanna do it yourself?"

"That ain't even a question, fam, Just give me the address. I'm choppin' the whole house down."

Chapter 5

The floor beneath his black Air Force One sneakers seemed to be made of clouds, though it was solid enough to support the weight of him and the two men he was standing between. They were on a white balcony high up in the sky, surrounded by glorious, thick, white clouds. The sun shined bright like a diamond forty or fifty feet to the right of them. Before them lay a vast city of black glass mansions and golden streets.

The man in the middle was Bulletface.

To his left stood Tupac Amaru Shakur, and to his left, Christopher "The Notorious B.I.G." Wallace. Like Blake, they donned black t-shirts over loose-fitting black jeans and Nikes, only their Air Force Ones were made of gold. He wondered why.

"You'll get your golden kicks soon enough," Tupac said, slapping a hand onto Blake's shoulder. "Don't rush it. You're the best thing the rap game's ever had. We don't wanna see you up here in Thug's Mansion until your time comes."

Blake became tense as gunshots boomed from somewhere below. He peered over the balcony... and suddenly he was staring into the windshield of a white BMW SUV. There were four black male passengers; all of them were firing assault rifles at someone across the golden street, glowering coldly from behind the dreadlocks that curtained their faces.

"Yo," Biggie said in Blake's ear, "if you don't take care of your enemies, you'll be rockin' these gold shoes a lot sooner than you think."

Just then, Blake caught sight of the man the shooters were gunning for.

It was *him*.

The bullets were riddling his still-standing body, shaking him from side to side…

He blinked awake and realized the shaking and the gunshots were real.

Wide-eyed and frightened, Alexus was frantically shaking him by the shoulder, and a stentorian roar of gunfire was exploding from somewhere close by.

Instinctively, Blake snapped to his side of the bed and simultaneously picked up the television remote from the bedside table and the gold-plated AK-47 he'd left standing against it. He aimed the remote at their 100-inch flat screen TV and thumbed down the power button just as the gunfire stopped, replaced by the screeching of tires.

"I'm killing someone tonight if that's not my men out there shooting," Alexus said, unhooking her own golden assault rifle—an M-16—from the wall above their headboard.

As soon as the TV was on, Blake went to the surveillance monitors, which were connected to the twenty-three cameras attached to the roof of the mansion. He had to rewind two of the cameras to locate the gunman.

The shooting had occurred just outside the wrought-iron gates at the end of their driveway.

A dark-skinned man with dreadlocks had pulled up in a white Hummer at 1:07am. By 1:08, he was standing in front of the Hummer with the barrel of his assault rifle ablaze as he unleashed a barrage of rounds at the mansion. He was back in the driver's seat and speeding away within sixty seconds.

"Zoom in on his face," Alexus said, squinting as she walked closer to the TV. "I've seen him before."

"Yeah, I have too." Blake zoomed in on the gunman's coal-black face. "That's one of T-Walk's guys."

"His name's Ant," Alexus said, nodding her head. "I've seen him with T-Walk on numerous occasions. I'm pretty sure he said he was from Gary, Indiana. You know how they are. Put a hundred grand on his head and let the streets handle him."

"Nah. We'll go out and find this nigga Ant. Pick me out an outfit. A black t-shirt, black jeans, those black Air Force Ones, and my white diamond MBM chains." The dream was still vivid in Blake's mind. He picked up his iPhone5 from the charging pad he shared with Alexus and phoned Rube, one of Gary's most trigger-happy Vice Lords.

Alexus protested, "It's one-ten in the morning, Blake. We just got to bed barely an hour ago." But then her attention was redirected from Blake to her phone's screen; Enrique was calling her.

Rube answered, "What up, lil bruh?"

"You know a nigga named Ant? Got a white Hummer?"

"Yeah, I did some time wit' dude, behind the wall in Michigan City. As a matter of fact, my lil cousin Shauntine just texted me a lil while ago sayin' she was at the beach in Michigan City wit' them Miller Project niggas. Why? What's the thought?"

"I'll tell you tomorrow," Blake said, and hung up.

It was hardly a quarter past one o'clock in the morning and Blake was getting ready to go to his hometown's pristine swath of beach.

He was ready to wet a motherfucker up on the shores of Lake Michigan.

Chapter 6

"You sure this five *hundred* kilos? Doesn't look like it to me," T-Walk said, blowing Kush smoke out of his nostrils like a raging bull and staring at the cellophane-wrapped slabs of cocaine.

The two mulatto-looking men stood behind one of the two U-Haul trucks that were idling in the parking lot outside the rear exit of The Visionary Lounge.

Inside the second U-Haul was $7.5 million in cash, bills of all denominations, packed into over thirty cheap, black duffle bags. T-Walk was paying fifteen thousand dollars per kilo. After cutting and selling the bricks for forty thousand dollars apiece to the drug-dealers he dealt with in Indiana, he expected to clear at least $22 million.

"It's five hundred," Cup said, his eyes darting around nervously. The parking lot was packed, but everyone was in the club, drinking, flirting, and turning up, loving the fact that some of Chicago's hottest rap artists were popping bottles in the VIP section.

Cup donned a jet black suit that looked just as expensive as the one T-Walk was wearing. The five-pointed stars and crescent moons on his black silk tie and matching pocket square were gold. Behind him, the rear exit door to the club was open. The inside lights were off.

T-Walk hopped on the back of Cup's U-Haul, pulled the door down and latched it shut. Cup did the same to T-Walk's rented truck.

"We've done more than enough business together," Cup said as they stepped back down to the narrow cement sidewalk. "You should trust me by now."

"I don't trust anybody."

"Feel you on that. Blake's my connect and I can't even trust that nigga. His bitch shot me all in my vest that night you and Blake shot each other last year. Then she put a hit on me and had one of my own Lords ready to murk me."

"She got money on my head, too." T-Walk had learned of the ten-million-dollar bounty the Mexican Mafia had on his head during a trip to Atlanta four months ago. He knew the order had to have come from the Costilla Cartel's top boss—the one and only Alexus Costilla.

The drivers of T-Walk and Cup's U-Hauls traded places and pulled off, followed closely by two blue 2015 Escalades and two black Range

Rovers. The Escalades were full of thuggishly comported Gangster Disciples, rich young dope boys with pockets full of cash and 30-round clips full of hollow-tips. They were T-Walk's soldiers and dealers, and he assumed Traveling Vice Lords of the same caliber occupied Cup's duo of Rovers.

"I just had my lil niggas shoot up that white Rolls Royce limousine."

"*Alexus'* white limo?" Cup replied, his tone replete with disbelief.

"Yup," T-Walk replied, lit that muhfucka up."

"That whole Mexican drug cartel is gonna want your head for that, and I mean that literally. They're the most ruthless cartel in Mexico, and they supply the drugs to not only La Eme, the most ruthless Mexican mob in all of America, but also to *every* gang in America. Ask those millionaire rappers that are *really* selling bricks, and I bet they say they're getting their dope from either the Mexican Mafia or the Costilla Cartel. They won't say it on camera because they fear losing their families over it, but they know. The streets know." Cup shook his head. "I hope you know what you're doing. This is chess, not checkers. If anything happens to Blake, I'll lose my connect and you'll lose yours."

"Chill out, bruh. Fuck Blake, fuck Alexus, and fuck that drug cartel. I'm war ready, nigga. I'ma do what Larry would do if he was out here. Run over these wannabe bosses and rule the streets."

Cup's uncertainty was evident as he kept shaking his head as he turned toward the door. "Let's go inside," he said. "Chief Keef just showed up about an hour ago. His whole team's in VIP, and their mad as ever about that Englewood shooting. They say it was an MBM hit, but I'm trying to talk some sense into Keef so we can keep the white girl flowin'. Same shit I'm tryna teach you. Don't ever make business personal. Just love the game and it'll love you back."

The sage advice went into one of T-Walk's ears and out of the other. As far as he was concerned, Blake *and* Alexus could die. Four months prior, Blake had murdered Bookie and Craig, two of T-Walk's closest friends. Blake had also killed Tasia, a beautiful New York native who'd been like a sister to T-Walk.

He entered The Visionary Lounge wearing a broad smile, eager to meet Bulletface's newest enemy.

Chapter 7

"I hope like hell we catch his ass out here tonight," Alexus said, sounding tired and irritated.

She was seated beside Blake in his matte-black Bugatti Veyron Grand Sport convertible, staring at his gelid expression as he steered the two-million-dollar car down Michigan Boulevard. Enrique was behind them in a white Chevy Suburban.

Blake didn't respond to Alexus' hopeful comment. He was much too busy scanning his surroundings in search of the white Hummer.

He was dressed as he'd been in the indelible dream: black t-shirt over black jeans and black Air Force Ones. The only additions were his gold-buckled black Louis Vuitton belt, his rose gold, white diamond wrapped Rolex watch, a matching quarter-million-dollar bracelet, and five long necklaces full of white diamonds set in gold, each with its own diamond-encrusted MBM pendant. There was a 40-caliber Glock under the Louis Vuitton bandana on his lap.

Alexus had slipped into a shoulder-less white Valentino dress and off-white Chanel heels that were the same color as her matching Chanel bag.

Blake had already driven around the beach thrice and was now headed to a gas station for the *5-Hour Energy* drink that Alexus wanted.

"Baby," Blake warned, "if I see that Hummer, just duck down, okay? With the top down and the windows up, you'll be safe. It's all bulletproofed. I'll stand up, blow all thirty shots out this .40, then it's over. You know I've done it plenty of times before. Just make sure you duck, baby. I'll take care of these fuck-niggas."

"Duck?" Alexus scoffed at the mere idea of ducking and drew her own 30-rounded Glock from inside her Chanel bag. If you stand up shooting, I'm gonna stand up shooting. Simple as that. We'll go out like Bonnie and Clyde if we have to, but I refuse to duck down while you're fighting to protect us. Papi taught me to fight, not to duck and hope for the best."

Blake shook his head, gritted his teeth cantankerously, and turned up the volume on an old Yo Gotti tune. *Cold Game* was one of Blake's favorite Yo Gotti tracks, and the sound of its drumming bass was soothing to Blake's soul.

Turning into the Duke of Oil gas station across the boulevard from The Swagger—the city's largest nightclub, owned by T-Walk—Blake cracked a smile at the blacked-out Lamborghini Aventador that pulled in behind him.

It was Young Meach and his fiancée Johnesha. Blake had phoned Meach twenty minutes prior and told him to meet him at "The Duke," knowing with a hundred percent certainty that Meach would come through.

"Stay in the car," Blake said to Alexus as he pushed open his door.

"There's no way in hell I'm staying in this car, Blake. Technically, we've been shot at twice in the last two or three hours. I'm the eyes on your back right now."

No need in arguing with that, Blake thought, emerging from his Bugatti just as Meach and Johnesha climbed out of the Lambo.

"Bruh," Meach said, "I just left Patrick Street. *Everybody's* out there, solid. Gettin' fucked up and pourin' out Remy for Yellowboy. I spent damn near four racks on a hundred bottles, but I didn't drink. That tour bus shit got me on high alert, bruh." He cut a glance at the 30-round clip that was hanging out of the pocket of his black hoody. "I'm ready for whatever, solid. Dub Life shit. Let these poles blow like Rio used to."

Blake chuckled dryly, cautiously flicking his eyes about the boulevard. He had the Glock in his Louis Vuitton shoulder holster under his left arm, its extended clip jutting out for all to see. Three more 30-round clips were attached to the side of the bullet proof vest he wore under his black tee. He'd gotten his license to carry a firearm in Indiana a few months before, and now he was thankful he had.

He glanced at the alleyway next to the gas station. Enrique's SUV was parked there with all of the doors ajar. Enrique and two more bodyguards were already standing around Alexus on the other side of the Bugatti.

"So what happened?" Meach asked, peering around just as vigilantly. "The nigga just pulled up in a white Hummer, hopped out, and got to blowin' a chopper at the mansion?"

"Shot up my damn limo," Alexus cut in. She headed into the gas station with Meach's girl.

"That's exactly what happened," Blake replied. "I saw the whole thing on camera, even zoomed in on the nigga's face. It was Ant, one of T-Walk's guys."

"I ain't seen no white Hummers. Come on, let's get us some Sprite. We off the Lean and Kush tonight."

Blake started off toward the gas station's double glass doors with Meach beside him.

Out of the corner of his eye, he saw a burgundy colored Impala full of boisterous young black women pull up to a pump, followed by an interracial couple in a rust-laden Jeep and a black Avalanche with darkly tinted windows and massive gold rims.

Obviously inebriated, the girls in the Impala—Blake recognized two of them as Kita, an ex-girlfriend of his, and her best friend Shay—pushed open their doors shouting, "Bulletface! Young Meach!"

For a fleeting moment, Blake directed his blinging smile at Kita. She smiled back, walking toward him rather quickly.

She hugged him and whispered in his ear. "Watch those niggas in that Avalanche. They're T-Walk's guys. I just met them at the club, and all they wanted was to find out where you hang out."

"Yeah?" Blake's smile widened.

He turned to the Avalanche just as Shay was moving in for a hug, snatched the Glock out of its holster, and opened fire on the Avalanche's windshield and passenger door, sending the girls scrambling back into their Impala.

Meach began firing at the Avalanche a second later, not even bothering to ask why.

Then the Costilla Cartel militants/ bodyguards started spraying the Avalanche with their FN-P90 submachine guns.

Whoever was inside the Chevy Avalanche did not stand a chance.

Chapter 8

"What are you still doing up, Rita Mae? It's two in the morning and you've gotta be at Harpo by nine-thirty. Get some rest," Neal advised.

He was lying on his back next to her with his eyes halfway open. Rita was sitting up in the king-size bed with her Kindle Fire HDX tablet in hand, reading Proverbs verses and sipping from a steaming Chicago Bulls mug of Coffee.

"I can't sleep, Neal. Not on nights like this. They shot up that tour bus while my daughter was on it. What if she'd been killed?" Rita's cotton-soft voice brimmed with worry. "There's a shooting every other day with Blake. Alexus isn't safe with him."

"Not safe *without* him either, with that aunt of hers still on the loose." Neal sat up grunting sleepily. "Alexus will be fine. Just get some rest. Call and have a talk with Blake in the morning."

"Talking won't do. Blake doesn't listen and Alexus doesn't listen, either. They never take heed to advice until it's too late. My nephew, Reginald—we all called him Bookie—was killed that day we were in Miami Beach earlier this year. And Blake's parents were killed on that very same day."

"I remember. One of Blake's friends got killed that day, too. It was the same day Tasia and Cereniti went missing."

"Flako's daughter was found dead in an LA junkyard that same night. I have good reason to be sitting here worried."

"You're worrying yourself over something you can't control. What's the sense in that?" Neal Miller curled an arm around Rita's lower back, pulled her tightly against his side, and planted a long kiss on her temple. "Relax, honey, there's nothing to be worried about."

Rita Mae Bishop sighed and adjusted her black-lace Victoria's Secret bra. She bookmarked the verse she'd left off on and went to a Terry McMillan novel she'd downloaded the previous evening, but then decided against reading and shut off the tablet. Another sigh followed. She sucked in about a teaspoon of Maxwell House, then sat the mug and tablet on the bedside table.

"I'm afraid for all of us," she said, crossing her arms. "Jenny Costilla murdered my ex in cold blood, shot him out of my office window. Well, not actually her, but she had her little boyfriend do it. You and I were nearly killed when she bombed my house four years ago. And let's not forget the time she nailed me to a cross and put a crown of barbed wire on my head. The last two men I dared to love were killed by the Costilla family. I don't want you to be next.

"I'll be fine."

"Don't be so sure about that. Jenny's the epitome of evil. She blew the White House off the map. Getting to you would be a piece of cake. I'd stay a million feet away from me if I were you."

Neal shook his head. "I've got faith in our military. They'll find that psycho Mexican one of these days, and she'll pay for all the pain she's caused here in America."

"I pray you're right."

"I know I'm right. Now lay down, will you? Get yourself some shut-eye before those bad-ass grandkids of yours wake up hollering like they always do."

Rita and Neal were in the spacious, white-schemed guest bedroom on the second floor of Alexus' fifty-million-penthouse at Chicago's *Trump International Hotel and Tower.* Its all-white décor felt heavenly to Rita Mae, and the fact that the penthouse was higher in the sky than any other Chicago residence made her feel even closer to God.

With a daughter like Alexus Costilla and a son-in-law like Blake King, she found herself needing God more and more every day.

Blake's eight-year-old daughter, Savaria, had her own bedroom and so did three-year-old King Neal Costilla, Alexus and Blake's son. Neal was right. Their bad asses would be up wreaking havoc before six.

Turning her back to Neal, Rita scooted closer to him. He draped a loving arm over her.

"The scent of this coffee's gonna keep me wide a—" Rita started. Then she paused as her iPhone5 began to vibrate on the bedside table.

Frowning, she sat up.

It was her brother, Dennis, calling.

At 1:54am?

Reluctantly, she answered the call. "Hello?"

"Long time no see, my friend."

A sharp gasp escaped Rita, and her eyes went agape.

The voice of the FBI's most wanted terrorist had a way of doing that to people.

Chapter 9

"I've missed you, sister-in-law. I really have. You're the only sister I have, you know?"

"What are you doing with my brother's phone?"

Jennifer Costilla smiled. She hadn't smiled in a while. She and her young lover, Miguel, were wearing the Chicago Police Department uniforms that Jenny had gotten made in Jew-Town for a hundred dollars even. Her Ruger pistol was in hand. Handcuffed beside his pregnant girlfriend on the living room sofa, Dennis was a diminutive brown-skinned man in his late forties. His dour expression bespoke his anger at having been awakened at two in the morning by the stern knock of Jenny's knuckles on the front door of his high-rise apartment, only to be cuffed behind his back and shoved onto his sofa like some kind of criminal.

"Get off my damn cell phone and tell me what the hell is going on," Dennis demanded. "If this is about that damn stupid ass ticket, I'm comin' to *your* precinct, you hear me? *First* thing in the mawnin'. And guess what… I'm *suin'* y'all's asses. I want every damn dime this raggedy city of Chicago got."

Although Jenny found his project English a bit comedic, she did not laugh. She heard Rita scream, "Leave my family alone! I rebuke you, in the name of Jes—" but she ended the call before Rita could finish the frantic and undoubtedly religious rant. Then she dropped the smartphone in her pants pocket and regarded Dennis with an iceberg stare. Her heart was bouncing off of her ribcage as it always did before she killed. She had gloves on—black leather ones—so as not to leave prints.

"Dumb hoe, is you deaf? If you don't get these damn handcuffs off me and my woman, it's gon' be somethin'. Get the *hell* outta my damn house. Come up in here lookin' like J-Lo and Casper." Dennis was becoming belligerent. Veins were bulging from his neck. Saliva gathered at the sides of his mouth. His breath stunk like shit. "What are you, a gotdamn Mexican or somethin'? *Let* me out the gotdamn handcuffs…"

Miguel said, "Please let me shoot him."

"No." Jenny aimed her pistol at Dennis. "Shut up and stand up. You and your girlfriend are under arrest. You have the right to remain silent. Anything you say can and will be used against you in a court of law. You have the right to an attorney. If you cannot afford an attorney—"

"What are you doing?" Miguel asked, frowning at Jenny.

"I've always wanted to say that," Jenny replied.

She pulled the trigger. Fire blew from the nine-millimeter's barrel. A hole appeared on the left side of Dennis' neck. Eyes wide, he slumped back into the sofa and slid down to the white carpeted floor; blood spilled from the bullet wound and created a crimson waterfall across his hairy bare chest.

Jenny's aim moved to the pregnant woman. She was dark and unattractive, and she yelped in horror as she attempted to stand.

Jenny squeezed the trigger twice more. Both rounds punched holes in the girl's forehead. She was flung sideways onto the arm of the Aztec-patterned sofa, and there she stayed while Dennis writhed in agony at her feet.

Retrieving a razor-sharp bowie knife from a pocket on her belt, Jenny walked around the table and glowered down at Dennis. He was gurgling with a mouthful of blood, and his eyes were rolled up into their sockets.

"Your breath stinks like shit," Jenny said as she squatted and sliced open his throat with the blade of her knife.

Her attention shifted to the dead pregnant woman. Lifting the girl's purple Juicy Couture shirt, Jenny used the knife to cut open her stomach. The little black baby slipped out. Jenny grabbed it by the neck before it could hit the floor with the bloody fluids of afterbirth.

"She must have been at least eight months pregnant," Jenny guessed aloud as she sawed through the umbilical cord.

"At least," Miguel agreed. "Let's hurry up and get out of here. I still haven't delivered those kilos to Sosa."

Jenny gave an understanding nod. She lay the crying baby on the coffee table. Then she took a folded note from her pants pocket and unfolded it, laying it on the baby's chest.

She cut off the baby's head and watched it roll off of the table as she stabbed her knife through the note on its chest. Then Jenny calmly walked out with Miguel.

Chapter 10

"I was able to get the recorded camera footage from the gas station clerk," Enrique said through the speakerphone. "I destroyed it. We should be good as long as whoever was in that Jeep doesn't go running their mouths to the cops. One of my men copied down the license plate number on that Impala. We'll have them taken care of by sunrise."

"Nah, they're good," Blake said as he veered the Bugatti onto Patrick Street.

There were dozens of young black men and women on the dark street, and almost everyone had red plastic cups and bottles of Remy Martin in their hands. Older-model Chevy Caprice convertibles on 28- and 30-inch rims lined the street on both sides. Blake spotted several of his top drug dealers walking toward his Bugatti and Meach's Lambo as they parked in front of the house Blake owned on the corner of Patrick and Willard Avenue.

"What do you mean 'they're good'? We're not leaving any witnesses," Alexus said, holding her phone over the center console so Enrique could hear Blake's voice just as well as he could hear hers. "If the people who were in that Impala give you up for that shooting, you may be locked up for the rest of your life. We can't take that chance."

"I said they're good," Blake insisted. "They ain't gon' say shit. Let me worry about me."

Fact was, Blake had a lot of love for Lakita Thomas. He'd fucked her too many times to count in the past. She had actually helped him beat multiple murder charges a few years ago by having her guys in Gary kill the witness. Plus, she had warned him about the Avalanche. There no telling what would have happened if she hadn't pulled up at that gas station.

Alexus said, "We're on Patrick Street, Enrique, get here." She ended the call and sighed. "I wouldn't be a bit surprised if I woke up tomorrow with a head full of gray hair."

"Don't let this shit stress you out, baby." Blake cupped her chin in his hand and kissed her lips. "No worries. We've made it this far. I came nothin' to somethin' big. You came from somethin' to *everything*. We're the number one power couple in the industry. It's me and you, baby, me and you against the world. Like Pac said, 'All I need in this life of sin is me and my girlfriend.' You're all I need."

"I love you, Blake."

"I love you, too."

"Always?" Tears grew in Alexus' eyes.

"Always and forever." Blake thumbed away her tears and glanced at the smartphone in her hand as it started ringing. Her mother was calling. "Go ahead and answer that. I'm about to step out here and holla at my niggas for a minute."

Blake was bombarded with hugs from the hood girls and Dub Life handshakes from his squad of dope boys. He'd brought ten crates of hand guns with 30-round extended clips to the hood after his friend Young-D was shot dead in Miami earlier in the year, and many of the guns were present now.

"Nigga, we poled up. Any nigga ride through here gets it on sight," said Cortez, a tall, slender, brown-skinned goon wearing a black Dub Life hoody. He was one of the city's most infamous shooters, originally from Memphis, where he'd starred in one of the many GD versus Rick Ross videos.

Cortez had a .45-caliber Glock with an extended clip in his left hand. His brother, Blubby, stood beside him with an equally perilous Ruger. Tooter and Snottz—two light-skinned trapaholics with mouths full of gold teeth and long braids that draped down from beneath their fitted caps—held

.40-caliber Glocks, which were identical to the one Blake was holding.

"First Young-D," Tooter said, shaking his head. "Now Yellowboy, in the same muhfuckin' year. A nigga gon' have to get handled about that."

"Fuck Chief Keef," Blake said. Lord n'em from G.I. already shot up O-Block. What I'm on is some nigga named Ant from Gary. He pulled up in a white Hummer and put fifteen holes in Alexus' limo."

"We on that," Cortez said.

Nodding his head and flicking his eyes around the street, Blake popped open the trunk of his Bugatti and wen to it. Meach met him at the trunk.

Inside the trunk, wedged between two Louis Vuitton duffle bags, was Blake's golden AK-47.

Meach said, "Bruh, Johnesha just got a text from one of her buddies. She say two of T-Walk's cousins and some lil nigga named DB was in that Avalanche. All three of 'em dead. Law got the Boulevard blocked off wit' like thirty cop cars."

"Fuck them niggas." Blake holstered the Glock and lifted his cherished golden Kalashnikov assault rifle out of the trunk. "I'm done playin' games wit' these niggas. It's back to the old Bee Kay now, bruh. Dub Life or no life, you feel me?"

"Awready. Dub Life or no life."

The next couple of minutes seemed to play out in slow-motion.

Alexus emerged teary-eyed from the Bugatti, sobbing uncontrollably. She ran into Blake's arms, mumbling hysterically about her Uncle Dennis being dead.

"It's Aunt Jenny," Alexus cried. "She's back!"

Then the screeching of tires behind him compelled Blake to turn around and study Grant Avenue, still holding Alexus in a consoling embrace, and still gripping the handle of his golden AK-47.

A white Hummer had just pulled up in front of the J. Cooper Community Center, and behind the Hummer was a white Audi sedan. Their doors flew open.

Gunmen with bandanas covering the lower halves of their faces leapt out with their guns blazing.

Chapter 11

"Get in the car, baby!" Blake shouted, shoving Alexus behind him as he raised the AK-47 and squeezed the trigger.

He sent several rounds at the gunmen. Meach and Cortez started shooting, then Tooter, then Snottz and the rest of the goons, lighting the darkness with bright flashes of gunfire. Blake crouched low and ran halfway up the block, ducking beside parked cars before rising and firing more 7.62-millimeter bullets at the attackers. Under heavy gunfire, they scrambled back into their vehicles just as Alexus appeared at Blake's side and opened fire with her own golden gun.

"I told you to get in the car!" Blake shouted over the roar of gunfire.

Alexus ignored him and kept shooting, so he did the same, spraying the Hummer's and Audi's driver's sides as they raced away down Grant. Tooter and Snottz hopped in their Chevys.

"Catch them niggas!" Blake shouted heatedly. He grabbed Alexus by the wrist and sprinted back to the Bugatti… only to find Blubby lying in the street with two bleeding holes in the chest of his crisp white t-shirt. Several others were also hit.

"Get bruh to the hospital," Blake said to Cortez, who was already helping Blubby to his feet.

"Let's cut down Willard," Meach said as he and Johnesha rushed into his Lamborghini.

Adrenaline surged through Blake's every vein. Returning the AK-47 to his trunk, he could not help looking at the other wounded victims. A girl across the street was sitting Indian-style on the sidewalk, both hands pressed to the gushing hole in her abdomen. Two of the younger goons were limping to their Caprices. On the corner of Grant and Patrick, the unmoving body of twenty-year-old Aaron "AJ" Neves lay in a growing pool of blood.

Blake closed the trunk. Simultaneously, he and Alexus opened their doors and sank into the Bugatti's gold-stitched, black leather seats. Seconds later, just as the sounds of more gunshots shattered the silence, Blake sped off ahead of Meach, veering onto Willard Avenue. He zipped past 9th Street, stopped at the train tracks on 10th and glanced in both directions.

He glimpsed the taillights of the escaping Audi three blocks ahead; down 10th to his right, Totter and Snottz were racing after the Hummer;

and speeding up 10th from his left was an MCPD patrol car.

The cop made a right and drove past Blake, turning on his lights and sirens and zeroing in on the droves of people who were fleeing Patrick Street on foot.

Blake took off after the Audi.

"I told you to stay in the car," Blake said, glowering at Alexus. "You could've been shot."

"Well I wasn't," she retorted.

"But you could have been."

"But I wasn't." Alexus tucked away her gun in her Chanel bag and massaged her right wrist. Her hands were trembling but the shock of the shooting had taken away her tears. "I've had enough of this lifestyle. I'm done, Blake. It's already bad enough that I have to live every second of my life in fear of Aunt Jenny, the enemies of my cartel, and the media. For Christ's sake, Jenny called my mom from Uncle Dennis' phone a little while ago, and now he's dead. Then, in the middle of me grieving over the loss of my uncle, I find myself dodging bullets and shooting to protect you. I can't take it. After this CNN interview, I'm taking the kids and leaving the States for a while, with or without you. I'm fucking done."

Blake was only half listening to Alexus' emotional rant. They were on a pitch-black road behind Indiana State Prison, rapidly closing in on the Audi. He lowered his window a couple of inches and drew his Glock from its holster. Then Alexus spoke again.

"No, Blake. We have to get my mom and the kids. Aunt Jenny's back. We can't risk not making it home to King and Vari with her on the loose. She'll kill them if she gets the chance."

The notion of his son and daughter being in danger calmed Blake immediately. He slowed the Bugatti from one hundred sixty mile per hour just as it was nearing the Audi's rear end. He pulled over to the deserted left lane and waved for Meach to stop.

Just then, the rear passenger's side window of the Audi slid own. The face of the man who eased out of it pointing a long-clipped submachine gun at Blake was illuminated in the Bugatti's headlights. Even behind the dreadlocks, Blake was certain of the gunman's identity.

It was none other than Chief Keef.

"O-Block, fuck nigga!" Keef shouted as he opened fire.

None of the rounds hit the Bugatti, and with the Audi's driver still speeding up the road, Sosa was out of sight within seconds.

Chapter 12

Chicago 3:07 a.m.

Eighteen-year-old Porsche Clark could hardly walk when she stumbled out of Club Adrianna's on the arm of Antonio Connilly, her favorite of the four armed bodyguards who'd been with her and her big sister, Mercedes Costilla, for about four months. Porsche was high off of two triple-stack Ecstasy pills, a molly, and the Kush blunt she'd smoked with Mercedes. But it was the many shots of peach Ciroc she'd ingested that had her wobbling on her leopard print Zanotti heels. A warm breath of night air blew across her nose and brought with it the fresh scent of Tone's cologne. Porsche closed her eyes and flared her nostrils, inhaling every molecule of his fragrance.

All of the drugs and alcohol had Porsche's brain clouded, but she was alert enough to understand what everyone around her was talking about. They were all muttering urgently, perusing the web on their smartphones. Apparently, the Chicago Police Department and the FBI suspected Mexican terrorist, Jennifer Costilla, was lurking somewhere in the Windy City. Now everyone was in a rush to get home to their families.

Jennifer Costilla had already nuked Washington, D.C. The bombing vaporized the White House and every building surrounding it within a three-mile radius.

Needless to say, Chicagoans were on high alert.

Mercedes' blacked-out 2015 Mercedes Sprinter van was waiting curbside. Tone ushered Mercedes and Porsche into the van. Then he shut the door and sat across from them while the other bodyguards slipped into the blacked-out 2015 Escalade that was parked behind the Sprinter.

"Maaaaan, big sis," Porsche said, yanking her snug black Marchesa mini-dress down to cover her dark brown thighs and opening the laptop computer that sat on the table before her. "Your dad's sister is a gotdamned terrorist. She's like a Mexican Adolf Hitler or somethin'."

"The Costillas are not my family," Mercedes replied. She was gazing out of her window.

"Ummm… I hate to break it to you, but your name is Mercedes Costilla. Your sister's name is Alexus Costilla. And you aunt's name is Jennifer Costilla because your daddy's name was Juan Costilla."

"Shut the hell up, Porsche."

"Don't kill the messenger."

Porsche logged into Facebook on the laptop. She had 392 friends and a massive 1.9 million followers, the latter due to her being the little sister of Alexus' younger sister. Her Facebook friends were a combination of old friends, distant relatives, and wealthy black celebrities. Every single one of them had already posted their prayers and well-wishes for Bulletface and Alexus in regards to the tour bus shooting, as well as their fears of what the FBI's most wanted fugitive might do to Chicago.

"Sis, you really should call and check on Alexus. You know she needs somebody to talk to at a time like this," Porsche suggested sympathetically. "Stop blaming her for our mom being gone. It's not that deep. It was an accident, and we've been more than compensated for our loss."

"No amount of money can ever make up for our mother being killed by that damn cartel. And now my kids don't have a daddy, either. Alexus had our momma killed and Blake had my baby-daddy killed. I'm not calling them. Alexus is lucky I haven't killed *her* over all of the pain she's put me through."

"It wasn't intentional."

"Damn if it was intentional or not," Mercedes retorted, flipping open her own laptop. "My kids don't have a father. Momma's gone. Nothing can change that, Porsche. Not this Sprinter van, not the forty million she gave me when we first met—"

"That's a lot of money."

"And definitely not the two million dollars she wired me in January. She's a fuckin' billionaire. What's two *million* dollars compared to fifty *billion* dollars?"

"A lot of money," Porsche repeated mater-of-factly.

Mercedes sucked her teeth indignantly and went silent. She cast a vacant stare out of the large, tinted, rectangular window to her left. She had on a skin-tight Gucci dress that was black like Porsche's, and matching black Louboutin heels that were covered in gold spikes. With her flawless reddish-brown complexion and basketball-sized derriere cheeks, she bared a striking resemblance to urban modeling legend, Cubana Lust, only her eyes were a glimmering shade of green, and her raven black hair was waist-length and straight, impeccably groomed and pulled back modestly in a Gucci ponytail holder.

Porsche was surprised and a little dismayed by the depth of her sister's anger toward Bulletface and Alexus. In Porsche's opinion, Bulletface and Alexus were the best thing since fried chicken, angels sent from God to relieve her and Mercedes of their financial burdens. She and her sister were born and raised on the west side of Chicago, and they had been poor all of their lives. Then they'd met Alexus and nothing had been the same since.

Now they were success stories, young black millionaires. Porsche owned a hair salon on Chicago Avenue. The pink Bentley she'd gotten from Alexus was almost always parked there. Mercedes owned two more salons and several apartment buildings, including the one they'd been raised in on the corner of Lake and Lockwood.

"I'm worried," Mercedes said suddenly. "What if that crazy lady, Jennifer, comes after me? She's sent people to kill me before."

"Yeah, and Bulletface saved your ass. You should be thanking him." Porsche clicked on the NBC News link that her cousin Kayshauna had just shared. Her mouth dropped open as she began reading the article.

The headline read: *Mexican Terrorist Jennifer Costilla on the Loose in Chicago.*

The woman responsible for killing over 400,000 Americans in the year's nuclear weapons attack on D.C. is, according to an FBI statement released just minutes ago, in Chicago, Illinois, and she's already struck again, killing three—a man, a young woman, and her unborn child in what our source from the Chicago Police Department describes as 'The most gruesomely disturbing crime scene the department has investigated in decades.'

The murders occurred at a Hilton apartment in downtown Chicago, an area that is now locked down and flooded with FBI agents and other law enforcement officials. Police are urging all Chicago residents and visitors to stay inside until further notice. President Bobby Gore has deployed a team of 700 Army troops to the downtown Chicago area. No word yet on whether or not we should be on alert for another nuclear attack. But with the unprecedented show of police presence, Chicagoans are understandably concerned.

Porsche shared the link on her own timeline and told Mercedes to read it while she herself read it again. A part of her wanted to spread her legs and offer the handsome light-skinned bodyguard a glimpse of her clean-shaven pussy. But the Jennifer

Costilla situation had Porsche's full attention. Her sexual feelings toward Tone had to be put on hold.

"I wish I'd never learned that Juan Costilla was my daddy," Mercedes said. "Life was so much easier before we met his family."

"No it was not," Porsche argued. "We were dead broke."

"Money isn't everything. I mean, look at all of the people who've lost their lives dealing with Alexus and Blake. Momma's dead. Duke's dead. Craig and Bookie are dead. Tasia and Cereniti went missing in Mexico four months ago. Young-D got killed and Meach got shot seven times in Miami. Bella was found dead in L.A. Blake's parents were killed at Disney World earlier that same day. My father was killed. Blake and T-Walk shot each other. And let's not forget about me walking into that Michigan City church and finding Alexus' momma nailed to that cross. The Costilla family is bad luck. Sure, they have tons of money, but they're the most dangerous family *we've* ever been around. Our mother is *dea*—"

"Stop it," Porsche interrupted. She dug into her designer shoulder bag and pulled out a bundle of hundred-dollar bills. "Alexus has a whole lot of this, big sis. YOLO, nigga. You Only Live Once. We need to be on the money team. I bet Alexus is on her way to a bomb-proof mansion somewhere in Mexico right now. You have to let go of that hate. Alexus is a cool chick who gave an order to some cartel goons to take care of some Whitney girl Blake had been cheating with, and the goons went out and killed a bunch of Whitneys. Our momma happened to be one of them. Can't cry over that forever. We'll be rich and safe with her—for the most part, at least. And we'll be *well* taken care of. Think logically, Mercedes. You really should be on the phone with her right now."

Mercedes sighed and retrieved her smartphone from inside her bag, but it began to ring before she could dial Alexus.

"Who is that?" Porsche asked.

"The babysitter," Mercedes replied as she answered the call.

Chapter 13

A sinister smile stretched across Jennifer Costilla's face as the call connected.

She was seated next to her boyfriend Miguel in the back seat of a black Hummer limousine, staring coldly at the hog-tied bodies of eighteen-year-old Roberta Coldwell and Mercedes Costilla's two children, Baby Duke and Meyoncé Sky.

"I'm on my way home now," Mercedes said.

"No need in going there," Jenny replied. "Tell Alexus I want to talk. Sunday. The Omnipotent. No cops or your son and daughter won't be living the next time you see them, comprende?"

Jenny ended the call and tossed the babysitter's smartphone out of her window. Her driver was lancing the Hummer limo up Cottage Grove. She'd changed out of the CPD uniform and into a black Prada jumpsuit and heels. Her sunny blonde-dyed hair was parted down the middle. Her malevolent green eyes were glued to the babysitter's terrified expression. Briefly, she wondered if the eyes of the two blindfolded children were as replete with fear as the babysitter's. She might have asked them if they were afraid had their mouths not been taped shut.

The babysitter's mouth was also duct-taped. No blindfold, though, for Jenny wanted her to see… all the way up until her very last breath.

"If these guys start shooting at us," Miguel said, his attention shifting sporadically from window to window, "I'm killing every one of them. I truly don't see how you can trust this kid. Isn't he on probation for pointing a gun at police right here in Chicago?"

"I believe so," Jenny responded.

"Then why are we even paying him? He doesn't follow anyone's rules. Who's to say he won't start shooting at us? Englewood is the most dangerous neighborhood this city's got. It's the reason why Chicago's the murder capital here in America. I say we leave him high and dry and head back to Mexico, or at least to Texas. We can sell the kilos for twenty thousand apiece in Texas, make off with four million easily. That's enough to—"

"No, Miguel. I am a woman of my word. I offered two hundred kilos for that tour bus attack, and that is what I will pay. Not a gram less, not a gram more."

The two hundred kilos of coke were hidden inside of a secret compartment underneath the limousine. For years, the Costilla Cartel had been utilizing their chain of limousine companies to discreetly transport their drugs from state to state.

Jenny took a deep breath; in through her nose, out through her mouth. The face of Jennifer Costilla was currently being broadcasted on every news channel in the country. They were using the mugshot from when she'd been arrested and jailed on Guantanamo Bay's military prison four years prior.

The mugshot looked nothing like her now. Jenny had undergone a total of twenty-three surgical procedures over the past four months, including two full facial reconstructive surgeries that had her looking more like a Mexican Joan Rivers than the terrorist the FBI was searching so diligently for.

"Still," Miguel continued, "you're paying this kid and he didn't even kill the Bulletface guy."

"Keef has the most dangerous gang of black gangsters in this country. We need more guys like him on our side."

"But we've got twelve thousand men in Mexico. They're all killers," Miguel argued.

"Yes. But we need more," Jenny replied.

Chapter 14

Thanks to the Bugatti Veyron Super Sport's W-16 engine, the drive from Michigan City to Chicago had taken less than forty minutes. It had been a silent ride for the most part, interrupted only by the incessant ringing of their smartphones as their family and friends phoned them out of concern. When Blake and Alexus walked through the door of the Trump penthouse, followed closely by Enrique and a phalanx of vigilant bodyguards, they found Rita sitting next to Neal on the living room sofa, gazing with teary eyes at her Kindle tablet.

"Get the kids up and dressed," Alexus said to Tamera, her assistant who was standing by the fireplace with Dr. Melonie Farr, the family therapist.

Not wanting to ne around the ex-cop, Blake shadowed Tamera into his daughter Savaria's bedroom.

"I don't know how you and Alexus haven't gone crazy," Tamera said as Blake pulled back the covers and sat beside his eight-year-old.

"I ain't worried about none of that shit." He gave Vari's shoulder a gentle rub. "Long as my kids are good, I'm good."

Tamera shook her head. She was a pretty brown-skinned girl in her mid-twenties. Formerly a waitress and sometimes-dancer at a local strip club, she was now Alexus' personal assistant, making upwards of $50,000 per month. Blake already liked her. She wasn't a conniving snake like Alexus' old friends.

While Tamera went to Savaria's walk-in closet to pack a suitcase, Blake watched his beautiful little girl sleep. The pink pony barrettes in her hair matched her bed sheets and just about everything else in her bedroom. Her eyes were twitching around behind their lids and she was frowning. Dreaming.

"Wake up, Vari," Blake murmured softly. She didn't budge, so he poked a thumb into her ribcage.

Her eyelids fluttered open just as he was planting a kiss on her forehead. She sat up, half asleep, twisting her balled fists against her eyes. She looked so much like her mother, Ashley Joy, who'd been killed during a kidnapping years before.

"Daddy," she said, stretching out the word as she reached out and hugged him. She slumped the side of her face onto his shoulder and again her eyes went shut. "I'm sleepy," she said, once again stretching the words out.

"You gotta get up, baby girl. We're gettin' on the plane."

"I don't wanna. I'm tired."

"We have to. You can sleep in the van, and on the plane."

"Well, carry me," she whined, barely audible.

Blake grinned and lifted Vari onto his hip as he stood. Seconds later, Alexus walked in from the hallway holding their sleeping three-year-old son against her chest. There were tears in her eyes, but her expression was calm.

"Just talked to Mercedes," she said. "Aunt Jenny's struck again. Baby Duke and Meyoncé are missing, so's the babysitter. Aunt Jenny called her, too."

"What'd she say?"

"She wants to talk to me. Sunday. At the Omnipotent."

"The what?"

"The omnipotent. It's the mega-yacht my father had built. Uncle Flako used it last. It's docked out in Malibu, not far from the money mansion."

The money mansion was essentially the Costilla Cartel's bank vault, a sprawling hilltop palace on the exclusive Pacific Coast Highway in Malibu, California, where over seventy billion dollars in drug money was stored.

"I told Mercedes not to mention the yacht to the cops, but I don't know if she'll listen. She sounded hysterical." Alexus sat on the bed. "I'm terrified, Blake. I really am."

"We'll be okay, baby," Blake replied soothingly.

He didn't even believe himself.

Chapter 15

The Gulfstream 650 private jet got them to Miami in two hours flat and they were at the Versace mansion in Miami Beach by 7:00 a.m. eastern time.

King Neal and Savaria had slept through the entire flight and were wide awake when they entered the mansion. Tamera agreed to watch them while everyone else headed off to bed. Blake and Alexus were fast asleep within minutes.

They were awakened four hours later by a knock at the bedroom door.

"Alexus? You up in there?" It was Tamera.

Just then, Blake's smartphone began ringing on his bedside table. Without opening his eyes, he slung an arm over to the table and grabbed the phone. Alexus rolled over and lay her head on his strong chest.

"I am now," Alexus said in a groggy voice that was loud enough for her assistant to hear.

"Your glam squad just walked in and CNN's camera crew got here about twenty minutes ago. They're unpacking their equipment as we speak. From what I understand, Anderson Cooper should be arriving any minute now. I know the interview is still hours away, but you need to be getting ready. Oh, and Harvey from TMZ wants to know if you would mind calling in at 3:00 for TMZ Live. They're gonna be discussing the tour bus shooting and your aunt."

Blake finally cracked open his eyes and squinted at his iPhone5. French Montana was calling but it ended before Blake could move his thumb to answer it.

"I'll be out in thirty minutes," Alexus said to Tamera. She eased back a little. Her pinky fingernail traced the bullet scars on the right side of his jaw. Her eyelids seemed heavy. "Who was that calling?"

"French. I was supposed to record a verse for him the other day so he can perform it wit' me at the Madison Square Garden show tonight."

"I'm sure he'll be able to understand you not being able to record it at a time like this."

Shaking his head and sitting up, Blake tapped on the missed call and put the phone to his ear. Alexus pushed down the black and gold Versace covers and slipped a hand into his boxers. His twelve-inch phallus was fully erect, bulging out like a concealed pole underneath the fine black fabric. By the time French Montana answered, Alexus was already pumping Blake's pole in and out of her mouth.

"What up, my nigga?" Blake grumbled.

"What happened in Chicago? You good, yo? You and Keef need to squash that shit before one o' y'all end up dead, my nigga. Focus on getting' this money."

"I ain't squashin' shit. We on that."

French laughed. "Y'all niggas is wild. Just don't light up New York tonight. I heard he's supposed to be in town, too, recordin' somethin' wit' Lady Gaga."

"Nigga, I ain't worried 'bout nothin'," Blake said, taking a line from one of French Montana's most popular songs. "I'll have that verse done and sent to you within the next few hours. Tell Durk I'll have that verse for him, too."

"No doubt, yo. Catch you at the show."

"One hun'ed," Blake said and ended the call.

His dick was already slathered in saliva and Alexus was sucking him tightly. He was tired but her oral skills were as eye-opening as a strong cup of Folgers. He had seven more missed calls—one from Meach, one from Kenneth Lerone, MBM's music manager, one from his older brother Terrence, who managed the record company from his thirty-million-dollar penthouse in New York, one from his club-hopping partner, Floyd "Money" Mayweather, Jr., and three from his daughter's mobile phone. There were four new voicemails. Meach's was first:

"Man, bruh, that nigga T-Walk posted a pic on Instagram about a hour before all dat shit popped off in the hood. He was in VIP at the Visionary Lounge wit' Cup and Chief Keef." Meach paused and then continued, *"Why did you let dat nigga slide last night? I ain't never heard of you lettin' a nigga slide. Lil AJ got killed, nigga."* He took a second, longer pause before finishing up. *"Fall back and let me handle it. Hit me when you get up. Solid."*

The second message was from the music manager:

"Just making sure you're ready for tonight's performance. I heard about the tour bus shooting. I, uh... hope you're alright. Yellowboy was a good kid. He didn't deserve to go out like that. I can understand if you're not up to the performance, but I believe it's imperative that you show up and show

out. This is Madison Square Garden we're talking about here. Do it for Yellowboy and Young-D. Do it for your parents. Keep going until the day you join them. The world is waiting to see what Bulletface will drop next. Live relentlessly. Forget all the drama and focus on putting out more material, on bettering not only Bulletface but also Money Bagz Management as a whole. You're an icon... the only two beings powerful enough to stop you are you and God. Call me when you get this."

Kenneth's galvanizing voicemail message put a determined grin on Blake's face. He set the smartphone back on the table without listening to the last two messages. For a while he watched Alexus as she effortlessly sucked his dick in and out of her throat. She began shaking her thighs, like a stripper does, and Blake found himself thanking God for creating Pinky the Pornstar, from whom Alexus had learned all of her moves.

She swung a knee over his head and again wiggled her thighs as she lowered her pussy to his hungry mouth. Flicking the tip of his tongue on her clitoris and rubbing his veiny black hands all over her pinguid butt cheeks, Blake inhaled the delectable scent of her juicy center before canting his head back for a taste. Then he was right back to tonguing her clit, while Alexus battering-rammed the rear of her throat with the crown of his thick black penis.

He felt the volcanic broiling of the semen in his scrotum an instant before it erupted into Alexus' steadily slurping mouth, spurting and gushing and oozing so heavily that she had to swallow thrice to get it all down.

Then came the sharp slapping of the palms of King Neal's hands on the outside of their bedroom door. It was his signature knock.

"Ma, are you *ever* gonna wake up?"

Alexus laughed as she got out of bed and disappeared into her massive walk-in closet. Two seconds later, she reappeared wearing a Louis Vuitton robe she'd gotten from her father years ago.

"We'll be out in a few," she said, unlocking and opening the door. "Let me and daddy get cleaned up first—"

King Neal ran past Alexus and leaped onto the bed with Blake, smiling widely and wrapping his little arms around Blake's neck. Alexus put her hands on her hips and regarded their son with a disdainful squint. Savaria walked in and stopped in the doorway, not once looking up from her iPhone5.

"Daddy," King Neal said, "Grandma made us some nasty pancakes that tasted like nasty food."

"No they did not," Vari refuted.

"Yuh-huh. They was so nasty I throwed up, daddy."

"No you did not."

Blake's head fell back in laughter.

"I did throwed up, daddy. Just like I did when I was sick that one time. Grandma got the nastiest food ever and Vari only like it because *she's* nasty."

Savaria rolled her eyes and sucked her teeth. "Daddy, can I *please* beat him up? Just give me one minute wit' his lil butt."

Blake and Alexus laughed. Heading into the bathroom, Alexus said, "I'm about to take a shower. Turn on the news and see what's going on in Chicago. No telling what that crazy lady is up to."

I don't even wanna know, Blake thought as he picked up the TV remote and turned on their 90-inch flat-screen. He figured nine times out of ten Jennifer Costilla had already killed again.

He was correct.

Chapter 16

"…here in the Englewood neighborhood where the decapitated bodies of a young woman and two small children were found a little over an hour ago. It is believed that Mexican terrorist, Jennifer Costilla, committed the grisly triple-murder shortly after killing three others at a Hilton apartment late last night. As you can see behind me, the FBI is out in full force, as well as…"

Jenny looked away from the iPad on her lap and studied the big-bellied black man as he placed an ice-filled glass on the coffee table in front of her. He licked and then bit his lip as he set down a second glass of ice for Miguel, who sat close to Jenny's right side on the faux leather sofa. The man's name was Daniel McFarland, according to his *match.com* page. He'd been in search of a black swinger couple but had hastily accepted the offer of a threesome with the attractive Mexican couple, which explained his attire—small black underwear and socks was all he wore—and the bottle of Ciroc in his hand.

He filled Jenny and Miguel's glasses, poured a third for himself, and extended his glass for a toast.

"To a morning of blissful sex with the hottest Hispanic couple in the city of Chicago."

Jenny and Miguel raised their glasses and clinked them against Daniel's. Though Jenny hated the word "Hispanic," she forced an appreciative expression. She kissed Miguel on the mouth, and then stood and removed her dress, revealing her nude brown body to the big black stranger. She spun around, watching him take in her every curve.

It was all too much for Miguel. He stood up, downed his drink, drew a silenced .45-caliber revolver from inside his Armani suit jacket, and shot fifty-year-old Daniel McFarland high in the chest. The big guy stumbled rearward, eyes wide. His glass hit the hardwood floor and broke into several pieces, and he joined it a half-second later. Miguel stepped around the table and pumped two more rounds into Daniel's heaving chest.

"Well, that was no fun," Jenny said.

"I hate Americans,"

"So do I, but we could have enjoyed the guy a little while longer."

"Did you see the way he looked at me? Nothing enjoyable about that."

"You were jealous, weren't you?"

"Jealous?" Miguel scoffed. "Jealous of this fat fuck?" He aimed his gun at the blood-bubble that Daniel had just gurgled up between his lips and shot a bullet through it.

Daniel McFarland died instantly. His brains exploded out of the back of his head like a meaty red soup.

With a malevolent smirk, Jenny crossed the room to Daniel's living room window. The sound of her six-inch Prada heels clicking across the hardwood was pleasing for some reason. They were in the third floor apartment of a Gold Coast building, next door to Mercedes Costilla's lavish home.

Jenny peeked through the blinds.

The street below was packed from end to end with CPD officers and FBI agents, but Jenny only looked at her niece's shiny, black Sprinter van.

"She's still inside." Jenny walked back to the sofa, sat down, and began massaging her clitoris with the fingertips of one hand while squeezing her breasts with the other. "I love you, Miguel. There's no need in being jealous. I wouldn't have fucked this guy if he were the last man on the planet."

Miguel laughed. "I wasn't jealous," he said.

"Sure you weren't."

"I really wasn't."

"Whatever. Just cut off his head."

Jenny was still rubbing her clitoris. She started moaning as Miguel pulled a hunting knife from inside his suit jacket and cut into the dead man's throat. It took him about a minute or two to saw through the neck. He lifted the dripping head with both hands and presented it to Jenny the way the baboon had presented baby Simba to the animal kingdom in *The Lion King*.

Jenny trembled in orgasm.

Chapter 17

Special Agent Josh Sneed addressed his FBI colleagues in an authoritative tone:

"Knock on every door. Ask them if they've seen any new Hispanic faces in the neighborhood, since yesterday evening. Take them in for questioning if they have. CPD, I need you all to barricade off every street for thirty blocks in each direction. I got a feeling Jenny's gonna come back for Mercedes Costilla. Let's get moving."

Running his long, slender, white fingers through the low-cut crop of silverfish white hair on his scalp, Sneed turned to the Mercedes van behind him and walked quickly to the rear passenger's side sliding door. He checked the big tinted window and then knocked.

"Come on in," came the voice of a young black woman.

Sneed slid open the door and stepped into the white leather luxury cabin, shutting the door behind him and settling into the sumptuous seat across from Mercedes, who was curled up underneath a heavy Gucci blanket, gazing vacantly out of her window. Her younger sister was sitting on a brown-skinned man's lap under an identical Gucci blanket in the seat behind her.

"She's not gonna talk," Porsche said.

"I'm trying my best to find Jennifer Costilla, but I'll never find her without your cooperation." Sneed kept his eyes on Mercedes while lighting a Marlboro cigarette. "Your aunt is a despicable terrorist, Mercedes. Terrorists do terrible things, like ruthlessly murdering children. Unless you want someone else to go through what you're feeling right now, I suggest that you tell me everything you know."

"We didn't see her anywhere," said Porsche. "I would have noticed if Jenny Costilla was around. We left the kids here wit' Poochie and went to Adrianna's, had a good time. She got the call from Poochie's phone as soon as we got in the van."

"And you're sure it was Jennifer Cost—"

"Yes. She said she wants to talk to Alexus Sunday on the omnipolar or something like that."

"The Omnipotent," Sneed corrected with a knowing nod. "It's that big yacht Juan Costilla left to Alexus."

There was a pause. Sneed smelled marijuana and liquor. He opened his mouth to speak… but was immediately silenced by an earth-shaking explosion.

Chapter 18

*'You niggas better go to church and pray to Lord
Christ*
*Tell ya families stay in the crib and lock your doors
tight*
*You'll hear some thunder, it won't even be a storm
night*
*Leave silver bullets in you like you been drinkin'
Coors Light*
I can't see backin' down... I got poor sight
*If your conclusion's I'ma start shootin' then nigga
you're right*
*Cause if your homies want some smoke, I'm on the
scene for 'em*
*See what this confrontation business really means
to em*
*I'll pull up on his block and spark the Ruger clean
through em*
*Cause speeches ceased wit' Dr. Martin Luther
King, Junior*
*I'll make it happen like Alladin, what's ya first
wish?*
You shot that and killed that, well nigga murk this
*You test the waters, I'ma teach you how to surf,
bitch*
*Great black sharks swimmin' right under the
surface*
Since I'm feelin' shady, I'ma curse til I slur spit

Fuck y'all bitch niggas, damn that talk shit and I'll make it happen'

Bulletface put the Kush-filled cigar to his lips and filled his lungs with smoke. Then he sipped a bit of iced Lean from his double-stacked Styrofoam cup and looked at his hundred-carat white diamond Hublot watch. He was more interested in the half-million-dollar timepiece's two thousand individual stones than he was in the time. The bracelet on his other wrist was blinging just as brightly, as were the large white diamonds in his necklace and earrings. He donned a black Louis Vuitton t-shirt with a matching belt and sneakers. His True Religion jeans were loose-fitting, and there was $30,000 in hundred-dollar bills in each pocket.

Blake was standing at he suspended golden microphone in his recording booth on the second floor of the Versace mansion, recording "Make It Happen," a track off of his upcoming mixtape, *The Bang Theory*, which featured Lil Wayne. He'd already recorded the verses for French Montana and Lil Durk. Alexus was watching him from the other side of the glass. His studio engineer was at the soundboard. Mocha, his leading R&B artist had arrived minutes prior with Will Scrill, because both of them were due to perform with Bulletface later, in New York. They were nodding their heads to the beat, all seated in black leather swivel chairs.

Right now, Blake King was Bulletface. He finished "Make It Happen" and moved on to the next beat. It had come from Kanye West with a $100,000 price tag, an ominous "drill music" beat with lots of heavy gunfire in the background. He'd already titled it "Bang Bang," an obvious diss to his new gangster rap enemy.

'All my niggas twistin' fangs, bitch, we gangbang
Got 30-clips in in all our bangas, pull up, bang bang
I'm from the Dub where all my niggas do is slang caine
And bitch, I'm plugged. My Chiraq niggas love to bang bang...'

Bulletface was just getting ready to freestyle the first verse when Alexus suddenly sprang to her feet, waving for him to come to her and regarding the smartphone in her other hand with wide eyes. He hurried out of the booth to her side.

"There's been a car bombing outside my sister's house in Chicago," Alexus said, reading from an NBC News article. "Twenty-one killed, eighteen more injured, all believed to be Chicago police officers and FBI agents. They were investigating the kidnapping."

"They think Jenny did it?" Blake asked.

"They *know* it was her. She beheaded my sister's neighbor the same way she did my niece and nephew this morning."

"Wow." Blake shook his head and sipped some Lean. "I don't ever know what to say. That's crazy."

"No, what's crazy is the fact that she's still on the loose in the United States. I don't understand how she keeps getting around without being seen. Somebody had to have seen her."

"Maybe she had surgery to change her looks."

Alexus nodded her head thoughtfully. "I wonder if the FBI has thought of that."

"It's a possibility."

"I'll ask that FBI agent who's always pestering me."

"Your mom needs to get that cop out of here."

"Neal Miller is not a threat, Blake. And he's not a cop."

"He used to be."

"Well, he's not anymore."

"We do too much on the illegal side to be havin' a cop around us all the time. I smoke Kush all day, and all my niggas sell dope. I'm not about to be hangin' around no cop."

Alexus rolled her eyes. The white, shoulderless mini-dress she wore embraced her every curve. It was Versace like her white diamond jewelry and croc-skin shoulder bag. Her snow-white Christian Louboutin heels were wrapped in diamond-encrusted spikes.

She looked at him and said, "My momma's brother was just *killed*, Blake. My niece and nephew are dead. Don't be so inconsiderate. She needs someone to hold her and love her at a time like this. And I do too."

"Don't do that." Bulletface displayed a tight grin. "You're trying to turn this on me. I just don't like cops, baby."

"Whatever. We'll be fine. Let's go out by the pool. I wanna talk to you before this interview."

Bulletface chuckled once. He told Scrill and Mocha to get a few verses recorded or written. Then he walked out of the studio behind Alexus, gazing unashamedly at her fat derriere. Small-waisted and steatopygic, Alexus had the body of an urban booty model. Bulletface loved ogling her from the rear every time he got the chance.

"What are we about to discuss?" Bulletface asked as they descended the spiral staircase. "Did I do somethin' wrong?"

"You're always doing something wrong."

"You don't be sayin' that shit when I'm—"

"Shut up, Blake. Don't get cursed out."

He didn't speak, just filled his mouth with Kush smoke and glanced at the two bodyguards who'd fallen in step behind them.

"Sometimes," Alexus said, "I wish my granny wouldn't have left me with all this money and power. It's too dangerous."

"It's a gift and a curse."

"Exactly. I mean, on one hand you've got it all, but you have so many people hating you for it that it's not even worth having."

"Fuck 'em."

"It's not that easy to ignore."

"Yeah, it is, just ignore 'em and keep it movin'. Success is the best revenge. Let the haters hate."

"You can't just ignore a person like Aunt Jenny."

"True. And I can't ignore Chief Keef."

"Yes you can. Your beef with him is way different than mine is with Aunt Jenny. She's a lunatic, a terrorist. You and Keef are famous rappers, loved by millions. You can avoid him by doing your shows and coming home to your family. He's not gonna hunt you down the way Aunt Jenny will."

"I'm not worried about him or your aunt."

"Well, you should be. I'm worried," Alexus said, dialing a number on her smartphone as they exited the mansion to the vast outdoor swimming pool. "Hold on. I'm calling Uncle Flako."

Tamera was in the pool with Savaria and King Neal. The three of them smiled and waved at Alexus and Blake.

"Daddy, you should get in the water with us," Vari suggested.

"Yeah, daddy," King added, smiling his father's smile.

Blake shook his head no. "Gotta be on a plane to New York in about an hour. Maybe tomorrow."

He sat down in the big white lounge chair next to the one Alexus sat in. Apparently, her phone call to her uncle had gone unanswered.

She sighed and looked over at Blake. "I'm nervous," she said.

"Nervous? For what?"

"The Anderson Cooper interview. I don't think I'm ready for it. There's too much going on right now."

"You can do it." Blake offered her the blunt. "Here, hit this loud."

"It's probably what I need." She took a couple of puffs, coughed a couple of time, and puffed again. "Yeah," she croaked. "Definitely what I needed."

"Get to the point. I was in there making magic."

"How many shows do you have left on this tour?"

"Why?"

"Just answer the damn question."

Blake chuckled. "Three, baby. Tonight and tomorrow night at Madison Square Garden, and then the MGM Grand in Vegas on Sunday."

"I want you to take a *long* break from your music after the Vegas show. We need to figure out where we're headed with this relationship."

"Where we're headed?"

"Yes, Blake. We've been on and off for almost four years now. It's about time we got serious."

He squinted at her and said nothing.

"Why are we not married, Blake?" she asked as she got up and put a hand on her hip. "Am I not good enough or—"

"Shut that shit up. We could've *been* gotten married." He snatched the blunt from her and toked on it. "You wanna get married that bad? For what? So the media can have somethin' new to talk about? So niggas on Facebook and Twitter can get all hyped up? I'm with you every day. I'm already your husband."

"You're not my husband until we're married." Tears welled up in Alexus' beauteous green eyes. "You know what? Don't even worry about it. I won't bring it up again."

There was an ashtray on the table between their chairs. Blake used it to extinguish his blunt. He pulled Alexus down onto his lap just as she was turning to storm away from him.

"Let go of me," she said, though she made no move to free herself from the grasp of his arm around her waist.

"I'm sorry, baby," he said.

"You sure are."

"When you wanna get married?" He planted a kiss on her cheek and pulled her tight against his chest. "We can go to the courthouse first thing tomorrow and make it official."

"Fuck you, Blake," she sniffled.

"I love you."

"You don't fucking love me."

"I do." He kissed her cheek again. "You know I do."

"Whatever."

"When you wanna get married?" Blake repeated.

"We have to have a wedding."

"Why? We can go straight to the courthouse and be married twenty minutes later."

"I want a wedding, Blake. It doesn't have to be a big wedding, a private ceremony will do. As long as I get to wear a flowing white dress and say 'I do' and kiss you to seal the deal, I'll be content."

Blake shook his head and grinned, inhaling the tantalizing scent of her perfume and rubbing a hand up and down her side. He remembered a few years back when Alexus wanted to fly to Vegas and get married without a wedding. Then she'd wanted a televised wedding. Now she wanted a private wedding.

Women, he thought.

"Fine," he said. "Set it up. I'll take a break from the rap game for—I don't know—five or six months, maybe longer."

"Thank you." Alexus pressed her lips to his and held them there for a lengthy moment. When their lips separated, she seemed happy. "I just want us to be married. I'm quitting the drug cartel business… for now, at least. My Uncle Flako can take the wheel for a while. He's been running the show in Mexico anyway. All I want to do is love you and take care of our kids until my very last day on earth. The way things are looking, that could be tomorrow.

Chapter 19

Two of the ten bedrooms inside of the luxurious Versace mansion were no longer bedrooms. One was Blake's recording studio. The other was Dr. Melonie Farr's office, and every piece of furniture in it was Versace. From the Honduran mahogany desk behind which Dr. Farr was seated to the white and gold leather sofa Rita Mae Bishop was lying on, to the matching curtains over the windows. Versace, Versace, Versace.

"I want you to close your eyes, take a deep breath, and hold it for five seconds," Farr said. "When you exhale, allow the pain of your brother's death to briefly escape with the breath. You ready?"

Gazing emptily at the high ceiling, Rita drew in a breath through her nostrils and closed her eyes. She listened as Dr. Farr slowly counted from one to five. Farr's voice was soft and soothing. Rita appreciated the sound of it. She exhaled, opened her eyes, and sighed.

"There you go," Farr said. "Relax. Breathe. You've got the floor. Tell me what's on your mind."

"I feel like Job from the bible, like God's taking away everything I love. My nephew was just killed right down the street from here not too long ago, and now my brother is dead."

Farr gave an understanding nod and jotted something on her notepad.

"Jennifer Costilla is the devil in the flesh," Rita said. "She's the most evil person in history. She bombed my house. She shot up my daughter's car and killed a bunch of innocent men and women on Interstate 94. She nailed me to a cross, detonated a nuclear weapon in D.C. that killed the president and nearly half a million others, and now she's out on another killing spree. What if she has another nuclear bomb? That's all I keep thinking. What if she manages to blow up Chicago?"

"I don't believe she will, Ms. Bishop. They'll catch her first."

"They haven't caught her yet."

"But they will."

"I sure hope so."

"I'm sure they will. The United States is the greatest country in the entire world." Dr. Melonie Farr leaned back in her chair, tapping the top of her golden ink pen on the middle of her bottom lip. "Hope you don't mind, but I looked at your net worth this morning. Thanks to Costilla Corporation and all of its subsidiaries—particularly MTN and MTN News cable TV networks—you've accumulated $4 billion, am I right?"

Rita Mae Bishop said nothing. Her eyes remained on the elaborately painted mosaic ceiling. She'd put on an asymmetric white Gucci dress to match her daughter's mini-dress, because she was going to be sitting next to Alexus on Anderson Cooper 360. She had a French manicure and wore a white diamond Tiffany tennis bracelet on her right wrist and thin golden necklace with a gold cross pendant.

"Yes," Rita finally replied, "sounds about right. Half of it came directly from Alexus. The rest I got from Costilla Corp."

"Why don't you get yourself a mansion on the other side of the world somewhere? You could stay there until Jenny Costilla's capture. It's not like you can't afford the vacation."

Rita shook her head. "I'm not leaving without Alexus and she won't go a day without Blake, so I'd have to get him to come along first. And I have to be here to keep Costilla Corporation up and running."

"You're doing a wonderful job."

Rita said nothing; her response was a morose nod of the head.

"You're a strong black woman, Ms. Bishop. "God won't put anything on your plate that you can't chew up and swallow."

"I just can't believe my brother's gone."

"Don't let the loss of your brother break you. Pray. Talk to God."

"I'm all prayed out," Rita said with tears growing in her eyes.

"There's no such thing as being all prayed out. God's with you when no one else is. Keep your faith in Him at *all* times." Farr scribbled down another note. "Are you aware of the Costilla's family's… business… in Mexico?"

"The drug cartel?"

"Yes."

"I'm aware of it. I think Flako and Pedro may still be involved in all that mess. Papi and Flako did time in federal prison for drug trafficking. I've always stayed away from that part of their lives. As long as they never bring Alexus into it, I couldn't care less what they do in Mexico."

"What if she *is* involved?" Farr asked.

"She isn't. Trust me. I know my daughter like that back of my hand." Rita wiped the tears from her eyes with the knuckle of an index finger and sat up. Her eyes fell on the extraordinarily beautiful psychologist. She wondered why Alexus was keeping such a stunningly attractive woman around Blake all of the time. It was a cheaters episode waiting to happen.

Dr. Farr eased forward in her leather Versace swivel chair, put her elbows on the desk, and clasped her hands together as if she were about to pray. She said, "Alexus Costilla is the top boss of the Costilla Cartel."

A long pause followed. Rita stared at the shrink with an incredulous squint. Farr leaned back and began tapping the pen on her lip again.

"Impossible," Rita Said.

"It's true."

"Can't be."

"I'm telling you, Ms. Bishop, your daughter is a cartel boss. She told me so herself. I looked into it just to see if she was pulling my leg. She wasn't kidding. She's the real deal."

"Is this some kind of joke?"

"No. It's the honest to God truth. Alexus is the boss of the Costilla Cartel. She didn't want me to tell you, but I feel like you have a right to know. She supplies almost *all* of the cocaine that comes into the U.S. She gets it from the cartels in Colombia, Bolivia, and Peru, thousands and thousands of kilos at a time. I believe she has somewhere in the neighborhood of two hundred thousand people on her payroll, from drug dealers and killers in Mexico to mayors and governors here in the States."

There was a second, shorter pause.

Then Rita Mae Bishop got up and left the makeshift office.

Chapter 20

"Mmmm… you're going too deep. It hurts… mmmmm… it hurts so good. Alexus dug her fingernails in Blake's lower back and gasped repeatedly as he continued to plunge his foot-long pole in and out of her wet pussy.

The two of them were going hard in the backseat of a blacked-out Escalade. Enrique was behind the wheel, and the two identical Escalades that were zipping up the highway ahead of them held Will Scrill and Mocha. They were all en route to the airport for their flight to New York.

Blake nibbled Alexus' bottom lip between his diamond-encrusted platinum teeth. He sank his dick as deep in her as it could possibly go and held it there. After a couple of seconds of that, his scrotum tightened. He pulled out and sat down, while Alexus re-positioned herself with her knees on the seat next to him and her head in his lap.

She closed her mouth around the crown of his dick and he erupted.

"Damn," he said, grunting as his love stick twitched and gushed a copious load of semen into her steadily sucking mouth.

Lifting her head from his lap while smiling and stroking his deflated phallus, Alexus swallowed and said, "All gone."

"Sick," lake retorted with a disgusted smirk.

"You love it, don't front."

"Triflin' ass."

"Oh, please."

"That's some nasty shit you just did."

"I'll be nasty for you any day," Alexus said, fixing her dress. "Besides, I can't let you get on a private jet with Mocha without getting a nut out of you first. Don't think I've forgotten about that little hand-holding incident on *106th and Park*."

Blake got himself together and pulled out his two iPhones.

"I know you just heard me," Alexus said.

"I heard you, baby."

"Don't let Bulletface get Blake King fucked up."

"Stop trippin'. Mocha is signed to Money Bagz Management. She's one of my recording artists. Nothin' more, a'ight?"

"I'll kill that bitch. I'm serious."

"And go to prison for the rest of your life?"

Alexus scoffed. "You really think I'll go to prison?"

"Anybody would for killing a world famous singer."

"Well, I wouldn't. I have diplomatic immunity. Know what that means?" She offered him no time to reply. "It means I can't be taxed, searched, or arrested. And that's under international law. I can murder that bitch and get away scot-free."

"Yeah right."

"Well, try me. Try me and find out," Alexus threatened as she wriggled her own iPhone5 out of her Chanel bag. She checked it and said, "Shit."

"What?" Blake asked.

"I got a text from Porsche."

"And?"

"They're flying here with that damn FBI guy, the one who put me and my mom in witness protection after Jenny tried to kill me on that highway. His name's Josh Sneed, I think. Shit."

Alexus shook her head and bit her thumbnail. "I feel so bad for Mercedes, but I am not trying to have the FBI all up in my face. I've told them I don't know a thing about what's going with Aunt Jenny. I'm not answering anymore questions."

"Why not? It's not like they can arrest you." Blake's voice was full of sarcasm.

"I'm not worried about being arrested," she said. "They'd never even try to arrest me. I know too much. They'd just kill me if they thought I was involved with Aunt Jenny's attacks."

"I'm not stayin' at that mansion wit' a cop *and* a FBI agent."

"He won't be staying with us"

"I really don't wanna be under the same roof wit' the cop. That's the same muhfucka who tried to charge me wit' all those murders."

Alexus sucked her teeth and muttered, "Just keep your hands off Mocha and bring your ass home after the concert."

"You ain't gotta keep tellin' me that. I don't even look at Mocha like that. She's like a sister to me."

"Mmm hmm."

"Why you wanna get married if you don't trust me?"

"Oh, I trust you alright."

"And what's that supposed to mean?" Just then, an exciting thought occurred to Blake, and he blurted it out: "I'm havin' a bachelor party! Damn, I had forgotten all about that." He turned to her, suddenly cheesing. "You set a date yet? We can get this show on the road. I'm ready right now."

"I can't stand you," Alexus said, and finally she smiled.

Her phone rung just as Enrique pulled up behind the other two Escalades at the airport.

"Who is that?" Blake asked, pushing open his door.

"My momma."

"Tell her I love her."

"Get out, boy. Call me when you land."

Blake stepped out feeling great on the inside but his expression was indecipherable. He wanted to kiss Alexus and say "Love you" but she had just swallowed his cum. So he shut the door and said it.

As expected, a crowed of arriving and departing travelers aimed their smartphones at the MBM recording artists. One of Mocha's four bodyguards grabbed Blake's luggage while she posed for selfies with several fans. Will Scrill's bodyguards weren't really bodyguards at all; they were cold-hearted gang members, Vice Lords out of Gary, Indiana, who had killed for him and would gladly kill for him again. Two of them—Rube and Batman—were dark-skinned with long dreadlocks, and the other two were equally dark and as large as NFL players.

Scrill was tall and brown, with a bald head and calculating brown eyes. He was at Blake's side as they entered the airport.

Blake kept quiet. He had four things on his mind: tonight's concert, the upcoming wedding, the undoubtedly epic bachelor party that would precede the wedding, and revenge against Yellowboy's killers.

Chapter 21

Thunder propped herself on an elbow and looked down at T-walk's face. His eyes were closed, but he wasn't asleep. The Beats headphones on his ears were plugged into the Samsung smartphone that lay on his bare chest, and he was nodding his head in sync with whatever song he was listening to. He'd pulled on his blue silk boxers a minute earlier, but Thunder was still nude. The two of them had just got finished making love on the fresh-scented hotel room bed. Thunder lifted the headphone off of his left ear. His eyes popped open.

"What are you listening to?" she asked.

"Chief Keef," he said. "Wanna listen?"

"No. I can never understand what he's saying."

"Just listen to this one." He took off the headphones, unplugged them, and let the song- "Chief Keef"- play from his smartphone's speaker.

"I'm high off this earth, boy… I'm where Jesus be
Shot a nigga ass if he don't believe in me
My strap super-fast don't think he leavin' me
Tray Savage got the Mac, he make it scream for me
He shot the crowd up, he thought he seen a G
Boy roll ya loud up 'cause you cain't chief wit' me.

*I got my nine tucked ready to let it meet a nigga
I'ma Glo O-Black ass nigga, I'll put heat to a
nigga...'*

"Why is he so damn violent?" Thunder
asked.

"That's how it is in his neighborhood."

"But isn't he rich now?"

"Yeah. He's still a gangbanger, though."

"He seemed cool when we met at that club
last night."

"That was only because he and I both want
Bulletface dead. When he left with his gang last
night, they drove straight to Blake's neighborhood
in Michigan City and shot the whole block up.
Blake was out there. One of his guys got killed. Few
more people got shot."

"Think all that had anything to do with your
people getting killed at the gas station last night?"

"Ain't no telling," T-Walk said. "You
hungry?"

"A little," she said

"What do you want?"

"I'll have a chicken Caesar, nothing too fatty."

"Guess I'll get a steak. And order a big dessert. We can share it."

"I'll get us a pie."

"That'll work."

Thunder's big black butt cheeks jiggled as she got out of bed. She sauntered naked across to the desk, perused the menu, and dialed the phone. She ordered a chicken Caesar salad, a sixteen-ounce sirloin, and a large pie with vanilla ice cream. T-Walk smiled at her.

"Twenty minutes," she said. "Let's take a shower."

T-Walk thought the shower was a good idea. He and his squad of Gangster Disciples were planning a retaliatory shooting against a clique of Vice Lords on the city's west side, a clique that was almost always with Bulletface whenever the rap star was in Chicago and felt like hitting the streets.

If T-Walk could not kill Bulletface, he would settle for some of Bulletface's friends.

Right after the shower, and the meal, of course.

Chapter 22

Alexus Costilla was in no mood for an interview when the interview with Anderson Cooper began.

The phone call she'd received from her mother at the airport had left her feeling alone and uncertain.

"Please tell me what I just heard from Dr. Farr is a lie," Rita had said.

"What did she say?"

"She told me you're… involved in the drug business. The stuff your father was waist-deep in over in Mexico."

"Don't believe everything you hear."

"Are you or are you not involved in that evil cartel business?"

"I'm not," Alexus had said, but apparently Momma hadn't been content with the answer because she and Neal Miller were gone when Alexus made it back to the mansion several hours ago.

Now it was 9:00 P.M., and Alexus was sitting in a comfortable white leather Versace easy chair in the foyer at The Versace Mansion. There were seven CNN cameras set up in front of her. Production assistants held furry black microphones over the heads of Alexus and Anderson Cooper.

"And we're live in five, four, three…" a producer counted.

Alexus took a deep breath.

Anderson turned to a camera.

"Good evening, America." His sage eyes shifted to hers. "And good evening, Alexus. Thanks for having me." He was on the edge of his seat in the big white leather chair.

She gave him a nod and a forced smile that did not match her troubled green eyes.

"Well, first off," he said, "I must ask the first question all of America wants to ask—How are things going between you and Buttletface?"

"We're doing great, actually. He's at home with me and the little ones most of the time. When he's not busy doing shows, you know, or making appearances. He's in New York doing a show tonight."

"How are the kids? King Neal's, what, two years old now?"

"He's three. Savaria's eight."

"Savaria's Bulletface's daughter from a previous relationship?"

"Yes. Her mother actually passed away when I was pregnant with King. She's fallen into the habit of calling me 'Mommy' over the past few years, but she knows who her real mom is."

"Can't let her forget that"

"No. Never," Alexus said, shifting in her seat.

Anderson cleared his throat. "I, uh, have a few questions in regards to last night's tour bus shooting."

"Craziest moment of my life."

"Were you on the tour bus when the shooting occurred?"

"Yes, Blake and I were in the bedroom when they pulled up alongside the tour bus and started shooting."

"I assume rapper Yellowboy was in a different room when he was—"

"Yeah. They were on the sofa near the front of the coach. The bodyguards who were shot were in another room."

"My God," he said. "That must've been terrifying."

"Definitely."

"Some are speculating that Bulletface's beef with Chief Keef may have played a part in the shooting. What do you say to that?"

"I don't think it had anything to do with Chief Keef. He's one of Blake's favorite rappers. I think it was nothing more than a couple of haters, or some of those crazy young guys who've been shooting people all over Chicago lately. Honestly, I just feel bad for Yellowboy's family. He has a daughter, and he was a nice young man."

Next to Anderson's chair was a black bag with CNN stitched into the flap in red thread. He retrieved an iPad computer tablet from inside of it.

"Just minutes after the tour bus shooting," he said, "this tweet was posted on Keef's Twitter account." He showed her the tweet on his iPad.

'HAHAhahahahahahahaha #RichNiggaShit'

"Wow," Alexus said, genuinely surprised. "It doesn't exactly mean he was behind the shooting, but it is—"

"Wait a second," Anderson cut in. "Are you familiar with Chicago rapper Lil JoJo?"

"Can't say that I am."

"Well, he was an eighteen-year-old rapper from Chicago's infamous Englewood neighborhood, and like BulletFace, he had beef with Chief Keef. The feud escalated on Twitter and ended with JoJo's death. He was gunned down while riding his bike down a south side street. Shortly after his murder, this exact same tweet"—he pointed at it for emphasis—"was posted on Keef's Twitter page. He claimed his account was hacked. What do you think of that?"

Alexus' mouth dropped open. She had planned to lead Copper away from speaking so much about the tour bus shooting, but he wasn't letting up. Chief Keef's incriminating tweet only served to make matters worse.

She shook her head, closed her mouth, and said, "I don't know what to say."

"I'd say the violence in Hip Hop needs to stop. It should have stopped a long time ago. These young black men are murdering each other like savages, particularly in Chicago, and it's all senseless violence."

"I agree."

"I'm sure you do"

"I do," Alexus said, "but all the blame can't be laid on the black inner-city youth. The lack of jobs in poor minority communities is a major issue, as well as unregulated gun laws, dilapidated buildings and houses that need to be renovated, and numerous other issues. I invested two hundred million dollars into rebuilding and renovating homes and businesses in Chicago's Lawndale neighborhood. Since then, crime there has dropped by seventy-eight percent. Shootings are down ninety percent, financial strength led to moral strength."

Anderson gave her a smile. "You've gotta be the most intelligent twenty-year-old—"

"Twenty-two," she corrected. "And I get it from my mom. She earned an MBA at Harvard."

"Have you considered going to college?"

"I don't see the need to at this point in my life, but who knows. I'm still young."

"Another question before we go to commercial break. Are you and BulletFace gonna get married anytime soon?"

A glowing smile grew on Alexus's face, but she gave no answer.

Chapter 23

*'I'm in love wit' the forty-fifty, I'm feelin' crazy
cause I miss my bitch*
*I want my baby back like commercials for Chili's
ribs*
Yeah I'ma goon, I ain't ever went for dat silly shit
*Step foot in my city, my semi spit, you'll be really
hit*
And I got pull like the trigga on the choppa
*To these bitches I'm a lover, to these niggas I'm a
doctor*
*Pull a Glock and phop a nigga's my meanin' of
surgery*
I'm the truth, you niggas daily committin' perjury
*All dat fake shit'll get you trapped in a deadly
position*
*If I clap ya neck'll get snapped and ya head'll be
misssin'*
*When you see me in all black, man you know my
plan is offin' ya*
*I keep the stainless steel dryers for you fabric
softeners*
*Then I'll choose the spot where I'll be tossin ya.
There chance of findin' you is like them findin'
Jimmy Hoffa*
*Are you mentally retarded? I say dat cause you
react too slow*

I move fast, got an afterglow… you niggas sleep on me'

The beat stopped abruptly.

BulletFace halted at the center of the stage and swept his eyes over the screaming crowd of fans.

There were over twenty thousand of them.

He brought his customized gold microphone up to his mouth and paused to catch his breath. He was shirtless with twenty gold chains around his neck. Thick muscles bulged from every inch of his sweaty upper body. A Louis Vuitton bandana hung from the rear left pocket of his sagging black jeans, and his sneakers were also Louis Vuitton. He spotted Tahiry and K. Michelle in the front row and acknowledged them with a wink.

"I love you, Bulletface!" Tahiry shouted, smiling her beautiful smile. Dozens of other women were screaming the same thing, but Tahiry's proclamation of love meant the most to Bulletface. He'd had a crush on her for years.

His breathing stabilized. He said, "Rest in peace, my nigga Yellowboy. MBM gang, nigga. This shit is forever. These fuck niggas can't hold us back. Money Bagz is here to *stay*, y'all feel me?"

More screams and cheers.

He sailed into an a cappella freestyle:

'My 12-gauge pump'll give you niggas brain cancer
And make you jump around like a Soul Train
dancer
I run through snow like Comet, Cupid, and Prancer
If you plan to rob me, you'd be kinda stupid to
chance it
I catch you on my block, I'ma blast all you bitches
off
Wit' the same strap dat' blew da last nigga's temple
off
This AK-47 piece'll fuckin' murk you
Have ya face lookin' like it's off the Reese's Cup
commercial
My peeps'll fuckin' hurt you, make you feel the
blazin' thunder
Since Jay-Z fumbled up under give me McGrady's
number
Cause I'm number one like Nelly used to be
And I'll leave a gapin' hole where ya belly used to
be
Plus, I went and copped me a box of Tec Shells
Diss me, you'll get popped like X-pills
I keep crack like a broke Easter egg shell
I'm aimin' so keep ya head still... Fuck nigga'

Head held high, BulletFace stopped rapping and showed his signature grin just as the beat to "Dope Boy" dropped. It was a song off *"The Bang Bang Theory"* that featured Young Jeezy and Lil Boosie.

The crowd went wild as Jeezy and Boosie hit the stage. Their excitement took Bulletface higher than any Kush blunt had ever taken him. He wanted this feeling to last forever.

Chapter 24

"And we're back with Alexus Costilla, live from the most elegant and expensive home in the country, once owned by the late Gianni Versace. What a beautiful home."

"Yes," Alexus said, flicking her eyes around the marble floored foyer and pinching her diamond bracelet between her thumb and forefinger. "I like the location. Right by the Atlantic Ocean, you know. Savaria loves it."

"Okay. Let's talk about your aunt."

"Let's not and say we did." Alexus laughed nervously.

"I know what you mean. It's an understandably troubling subject."

"Growing up in Brownsville, Texas, I spent a lot of time with Aunt Jenny. She would always take me shopping, and to get my hair and nails done. Girl stuff, you know. We flew to Paris a bunch of times. She always liked to shop there. I still have one of the Chanel bags she bought me when I turned sixteen. All the other things were confiscated by the DEA when my father was arrested in twenty-ten."

Anderson looked at his iPad again. His navy-blue suit and tie were impeccable as were his shoes. His eyes seemed overly inquisitive behind the lens of his old-fashioned horn-rimmed glasses.

"The FBI has reported that Jennifer Costilla is in fact responsible for the murders of your uncle Dennis, his girlfriend, their unborn child, your sister Mercedes' two children, their babysitter, twelve FBI agents, and nine Chicago policemen, all within the last twenty-four hours. Your family must be devastated."

Tears burgeoned along Alexus' lower eyelids. She pinched her bracelet tight and managed to hold herself together.

"It's unfortunate that someone can be so… evil." A teardrop went skiing down her left check. "Especially someone you loved someone you looked up to. But yes, my family is devastated. My mom's been crying nonstop, my sister Mercedes hasn't said a word since she got the news about her kids and I haven't talking to my cousin Kenya yet, but I'm sure she's torn over her father's murder. We all are."

Anderson leaned toward Alexus, took her left hand in his right, and applied a consoling squeeze. Enrique stepped away from the wall to the right of her where he stood among four other bodyguards and dabbed her face dry with a tissue.

A brief movement of silence ensued.

Then Anderson said, "You alright?"

She nodded.

"If you could say one thing to your Aunt Jenny, what would it be?"

"I'd tell her to turn herself in. I'd ask her to stop killing innocent people. I'd ask her where in life did she go wrong, and what is it that has her so angry at me and my family. I suppose I'd ask her a lot of things."

"You're a strong young lady, Alexus."

She nodded.

"I don't think I know anyone who's had as many family members killed as you have." He gave her hand another squeeze and then released it. "Do you fault the U.S. government for releasing her from Guantanamo Bay? I mean, here's a woman who was captured for terrorism and then released for a U.S. military prison, and now she's wanted for killing over four hundred thousand Americans. Should the government have kept her in custody?"

"I'm not pointing fingers. The leader of that ISIS terrorist group in Iraq was also in Guantanamo at one time. No one knows if these terrorists will straighten up or not. It's really a—"

BDDDDDDAT! BDDDAT! BDDDDDDDDDAT!

Fully-automatic gunfire boomed from somewhere out front.

Enrique swooped in and curled a stout arm around Alexus' waist. As he was snatching her up from the chair, she balled her fingers into the collar of Anderson Cooper's suit jacket and pulled him up with her.

"Good Lord," Copper said.

"Everybody to the back!" Enrique shouted.

The gunfire continued, illuminating the front windows in sporadic flashes. Enrique ushered them into a vacant bedroom while the other bodyguards drew FN-P90 submachine guns from inside their blazers. The CNN crew entered the bedroom seconds later, followed by Dr. Melonie Farr, Tamera, Savaria, and King Neal. All of them hurried into the walk-in closet. Vari and King flanked Alexus and hugged her tightly.

"You can't get a break," Copper said, putting a hand on Alexus arm.

"Sounds like a *war* out there," Tamara said.

"Ma, I'm scared," Savaria said, crying.

Enrique brought up the outdoor surveillance cameras on his iPhone and showed it to Alexus. Dozens of thuggishly-dressed Hispanic men were firing assault rifles at Alexus' armed bodyguards, both in front of the mansion and on the side street. They were taking cover next to cars. The bodyguards were returning fire. Bodies were stretched out all around the mansion.

"We've got twenty-four men outside," Enrique said. "Looks like we've lost about nine of them already."

"Jesus Christ," said Anderson Cooper.

Chapter 25

Jennifer Costilla was all smiles.

She and Miguel had managed to escape Mercedes Costilla's neighborhood by blending into the throngs of frightened local residents as they fled the carnage in the middle of their block. She had scampered past dead and critically wounded FBI agents and Chicago police officers, struggling to hold back the nefarious smile that now shown on her surgically reconstructed face.

"This has been one of the greatest days of my life," she said as she sat next to Miguel in the passenger's seat of the red Chevy Malibu. She was watching the Miami Beach shootout on her computer tablet and thanking God for her Mexican Mafia connections.

Miguel had just parked the car about twenty yards up the road from the Highland Park mansion they were there to visit.

"It has been a great one," he said with a chuckle.

"Yes. Most certainly."

"What if they kill her?"

"They won't."

"But you *told* them to kill her."

"They'll never make it past Enrique, and he's going to protect Alexus until his last breath."

"Then what was the point in sending them in the first place?"

"To instill *fear*, Miguel. To frighten the living daylights out of Alexus, you see? Frighten her away from the cartel. That way, my dear brother Flako can take over and bring the cartel back to its roots. Alexus is my niece, and I love her dearly, but she is an American. No American deserves the right to lead a Mexican drug cartel. My mother left the cartel to Alexus because she said her granddaughter was the only Costilla smart enough to inherit the family business and keep it thriving. It should have been left to *me*."

"Vida Costilla was pretty old, wasn't she?"

"Yes. My mother was seventy-three. She didn't know what she was doing."

"She couldn't have. Nobody can think clearly at that age."

"She was taken advantage of," Jenny said.

"Alexus should be ashamed of herself."

"She really should. But it's okay. She'll pay dearly. I'm far from done with her. When it's all said and done, she'll curse the day she became boss of the Costilla Cartel."

"I think she's already cursing that day."

"I think you're right," Jenny said, and her villainous smile returned.

Chapter 26

'I want from old-school Chevys to drop-top Bugattis
You and yo' nigga diss me, I'ma be done caught
two bodies
I'm worth about a billion, I got money to da ceilin'
Icy neck and icy wrists and icy grille, I swear I'm
chillin'
I can still whip up a brick and hit da hood and make
a killin'
But now I just supply it, I'm too rich to do the
dealin...'

The bottle of the Ace of Spades in Bulletface's left hand was half empty, and he was half drunk. But he wasn't too drunk to keep the lyrics flowing. He was performing "Brick Man", an older song of his that had been out for over a year and was still getting spins on the rap radio stations.

Will Scrill was onstage with him. He too was shirtless and wearing twenty gold chains, and he had just grabbed K. Michelle's hand and pulled her onto the stage.

Fuck it, BulletFace thought. He handed Scrill the gold bottle and then reached into the crowd, took Tahiry's hand in his, and lifted her onto the stage with him. She had on tight black dress and Louboutin heels. Still rapping into his mic, he ogled her incredible backside while she laughed and moved her body to the beat.

The show ended minutes later, and Bulletface soon found himself face to face with the Dominican goddess in a dark room backstage. His hands went to her famous bottom.

"We can't do this," she said.

"Yes the fuck we can," he quipped.

"No we can't. You've already got the most powerful woman in the world. Don't screw that up."

"We're about to get married," he reasoned, squeezing the fat rear cheeks. "I think I deserve to fuck somebody else before I walk down that aisle."

"You think so?"

"Hell yeah."

"If we did it right now, would you tell Alexus or would you hide it from her? Be honest."

He hesitated. "I'd tell her… eventually," he said finally.

"What do you think she'd say about it? And a better question, what would you say if she went backstage and did the nasty with *her* favorite rapper?"

"So I'm your favorite rapper?"

Smiling, Tahiry rolled her eyes and shook her head. The two of them were standing in the middle of the room. Chairs lined the white walls, and there were three small tables. Bulletface could hear what must have been forty or fifty people conversing in the hallway. He heard Jeezy and Boosie laughing just outside the door; he heard his brother Terrence say, "Is my lil brother in there with that girl?" The doorknob shook as Terrence tried to open it, but it was locked.

Tahiry had locked it.

"Doesn't Alexus have a sister?" she asked.

"Why?"

"Because she is going to be kickin' you like Solange was kickin' Jay."

Bulletface laughed.

From outside the door, Terrence shouted, "Blake! Nigga, open up this muhfuckin' door. We gotta go, bruh! Somebody just shot up the Versace Mansion!"

"Oh, my God, is he serious?" Tahiry murmured.

Bulletface's attention shifted to the wall-mounted flat screen television. "Open the door," he said, walking to the TV. His heart was racing and his hand was in his pocket, digging out his smartphone.

"I hope everyone's okay," Tahiry said as she unlocked and opened the door. Terrence rushed in, looking like a taller, leaner Blake in a business suit.

Bulletface turned the channel from Bravo to CNN, because he knew that Alexus' interview with Anderson Cooper could not have been over yet. His diamond watch read 9:34 P.M. The AC36 interview wasn't supposed to end for another twenty-six minutes.

But it was indeed over.

Anderson Cooper was in the back of a van on the right side of the screen. Dan Lemon was at CNN headquarters on the left. The caption on the bottom of the screen read: *SHOOTOUT AT THE VERSACE MANSION.*

"Yes, that is correct." Cooper was saying. "Eighteen confirmed dead so far, several others wounded. Alexus' team of armed bodyguards exchanged gunfire with the gunman until police arrived. The remaining gunman then returned to their vehicles and led Miami PD on a high-speed chase down Mac Arthur Causeway, where it ended moments later in a hail of gunfire. All of the gunmen in those two vehicles are reportedly deceased."

"And what about Alexus?" Lemon asked.

Bulletface held his breath and waited for the answer.

"She's been taken to an undisclosed location, but she and her children are okay. Neither of them were harmed in the shooting. She spoke briefly with police before…"

Bulletface turned and saw that the crowd from the hallway had spilled into the room. All of the recording artists who'd appear on stage with him tonight—Scrill, Mocha, Boosie, Jeezy, Twista, French Montana, and Yo Gotti—were staring at him.

He turned on his iPhone5 (he always turned it off before shows) and phoned Alexus while everyone in the room watched the television.

"It was Jenny," she said as soon as she answered. "I'd bet my life on it. T-Walk or Chief Keef couldn't have sent a dozen Mexicans with AK-47s. That was a Mexican Mafia hit. Shit, they killed six of my bodyguards and wounded twelve more."

"Don't even trip. I'm on my way to Chicago," Blake said, motioning for Scrill as he moved through the crowded room and into the hallway.

"We're at the Palm Island mansion," Alexus said

"Stay there."

"Be safe, Blake."

"I'll be okay"

"Put your vest on as soon as you get there, and keep an assault rifle within arm's reach. I'll have twenty men waiting for you at O'Hare when you land."

"I don't need no security."

"Yes you do."

"Nah, I'm good. Me and my niggas strapped up. I'ma catch T-Walk, Keef, *and* yo' auntie, and on my son I'm killin'em."

Chapter 27

'Middle Fingas to dat reggie, 'cause all I smoke is land
Dem guns super loud, we'll shoot a nigga down
We don't fuck wit' new niggas, so don't get screwed, nigga
You's a muhfuckin' sting and we robbin' you, nigga
You bulletproof, nigga? Then lace your shoes, nigga
We be blowin' like a fan, we'll let dat cool getcha
But dem bullets hit'choo hot, show no love fo' a thot
Or no love fo' a nigga if dat nigga wit' da opps
So... getcha top dropped, like a drop-top
Think you callin' the police, you gon' get a cop dropped...'

Chief Keef's "Aimed At U" boomed from the S600's speakers. The Mercedes was bone-white with darkly tinted windows. There were four men inside of it. Glocks with 30-round clips lay on the laps of their expensive designer jeans. Their Styrofoam cups were full of Sprite, Promethazine, and Codeine. They were coughing and passing around blunts of OG Kush.

Sitting behind the driver, Chief Keef was staring vacantly at his gun. Tadoe sat beside him. Fredo Santana was in the passenger's seat next to Ballout, the driver.

They were parked across the street from Madison Square Garden's parking garage exit.

"Soon's they pull out?" Tadoe asked.

"Nah," Chief Keef said. "We ain't got time for jail time. We'll follow 'em until we can blow at that fuck nigga and get away wit' it."

"On David," said Fredo.

"Turn on some Gucci," Chief Keef said.

Ballout changed the music to a Gucci Mane mixtape, and for a couple of minutes they sat and smoked and listened as Gucci described his collection of flawless diamond jewelry.

Then a white Rolls-Royce Phantom Drophead Coupe cruised out of the parking garage, followed by four more white Phantoms, a red Ferrari, a black Lamborghini, three blacked-out Range Rovers, and four blacked-out Escalades. A phalanx of black women who'd been lingering near the exit began running alongside the second Phantom, shouting "BulletFace!" and slapping the windows.

Chief Keef grinned.

Ballout flicked on the Benz's headlights and pulled off behind the motorcade of foreign cars and SUVs.

Chapter 28

"Calm down," Tahiry said.

"I'm calm," BulletFace said.

"No, you're not. Your jaw muscles are tight. Your hands are balled into fists. You need to relax. Your family's safe. That's the only thing that matters."

"I know. I'm good. I'm calm," he said.

But he was not calm. He was fifty miles from calm and an inch away from insanity. He was ready to board his Gulfstream private jet, fly to Chicago, and go on a killing spree.

Tahiry massaged his shoulders. She was next to him in the backseat of the Rolls Royce he'd bought last year to keep at the Waldorf Astoria where his twenty-million-dollar apartment was located.

"Let's talk about something positive," Tahiry said. "You had a good show tonight. I am so in love with the sound of Mocha's voice. That girl can sing her heart out."

Bulletface said nothing. He was livid.

"What made you pull me out of the crowd? Was it because Will Scrill pulled K. Michelle onstage?"

He looked at the beautiful woman to his left. "I lifted you out the crowd 'cause I like you."

"Really? How long have you *liked* me?"

"For a while."

"How long is a while?"

"Ever since I first saw you in Show Magazine. Think I was about seventeen or eighteen. I saw all dat ass and fell in love."

"Is that why you ended up with Alexus? She's got a big one, too."

He shrugged, "Might be."

"I remember watching the news one day and seeing a story about her dad being some kind of cartel leader in Mexico."

"Yeah. Papi was a muhfucka."

"And now his sister's a terrorist."

"She's a muhfucka, too."

"Do you think they have anything to do with all these shootings? They may be somehow tied to your parents being killed in that Disney World shooting. And what's up with you and Chief Keef? I thought you and him were cool?'"

"You ask too many questions."

"I wanna know. Everybody's scared of him, and a lot of people are scared of you, too. They say the two of you shoot guns like it's the cool thing to do. It's that gangbanging culture. I just had this conversation with Joe the other day. It seems like rappers in Chicago focus on shooting each other, while all the other rappers focus on the dope game. It's sad, really. I'd hate to see either of you die."

"Fuck that nigga."

Tahiry sucked her teeth and regarded Bulletface with a light smile. Her beauty was overwhelming. Like Alexus, she was sexy and steatopygic, the epitome of a dime piece, and he could not wait to get her alone in the bedroom of his spacious Park Avenue apartment. It would be his last sexual tryst and he could think of no better candidate. He was hoping for a quick nut before heading to the airport. With Jenny Costilla, Chief Keef, and T-Walk all roaming the streets of Chicago, he figured it best to enjoy his time here in New York first.

"Hope you don't plan on us doing anything once you're married," Tahiry said. "I'm not into that kind of drama."

"I wouldn't cheat on my wife."

"Sure you wouldn't."

"I'm serious. I love Alexus."

"But you wanna fuck me, huh? Just one time."

He grinned. "Yup."

"No man has ever tasted this and not come back for more."

"First time for everything."

She sucked her teeth again. Her smile returned. Her eyes moved to her iPhone5, and Bulletface's went to his window. He opened the curtain and gazed out. He wanted to call Alexus, but she'd told him she would phone him when she got King to sleep. He wanted to call his parents, but they were in Heaven, had been for four months now. He wanted to call Chief Keef and T-Walk to squash all the beef before any more blood was shed, but his pride would not allow it. He wanted to call his daughter's phone, but he knew she too was probably trying to get King Neal to sleep.

It was a warm night in New York City. Traffic was mildly congested, as it was on all Friday nights. People were gawking at the fleet of Rolls Royces as they traversed the city streets.

Tahiry said, "Everybody on Twitter is talking about the Versace Mansion shooting. They're all praying for Alexus. Nicki Minaj, Porsha and Kandi from the Atlanta Housewives, Lala, Rasheeda, Rihanna, Keke Palmer—the list goes on and on. I would put in my two cents but I don't feel right about it.

"Why not?"

"Come on now, Bulletface. You know why."

"No, I don't. Tell me," he said, turning to close the curtain over his windows just as a sleek white Mercedes pulled up beside his Phantom.

The Benz's driver's window slid down, and the door behind it flew open.

Bulletface watched Chief Keef get out of the Benz's backseat with a long-clipped pistol. He aimed it at Bulletface's window and opened fire.

Chapter 29

Two birds with one stone, Alexus thought.

She had told Vari to lay in her bed with King and talk to him until he fell asleep.

"Me and you can stay up and watch a movie once you get him to sleep," Alexus had said.

"Can I pick the movie?" Savaria had asked.

"Of course you can. Just get him to sleep while I talk to these policemen. Then it'll only be you and me."

That had been forty minutes ago. The "policemen" were FBI agents who arrived with Mercedes Costilla and Porsche Clark. The agents had just left out, and now Alexus was standing in the doorway of King's WWE-themed bedroom. His bed was essentially a wrestling ring, complete with ropes and *WrestleMania* turnbuckles. Depicted on the pillowcase were blue steel chairs, folded closed as they so often were when used as weapons in wrestling matches. Savaria and King were both asleep in the bed.

Alexus pulled the door shut and sighed. She looked down at the iPhone5 in her right hand and decided against calling Blake. She needed time to think. There was too much going on, way too much. Though Savaria was not her biological daughter, she feared for the little girl's safety just as much as she did King Neal's.

She turned and headed up the marble-floored hallway. Like most of her homes, the mansion's interior was all white. She'd purchased the 14,000-square foot Miami mansion for $31 million and had spent an additional $11 million on upgrades.

At the end of the second-floor hallway was an elevator. Enrique was waiting with the doors open. As Alexus made it to the elevator and stepped in with him, he said, "The chef's cooking a light meal for Mercedes. Her little sister says they haven't eaten all day. Meant to tell you that on the way up."

"I'm going down to talk to her now," Alexus said.

"To who, the sister? She's gone already."

"Mercedes is gone?"

"No, the black one's gone."

"They're both black, Enrique."

"You know what I mean, the dark one."

"Her name's Porsche."

"Well, she just left out behind those fed guys. Said she was going over to that party the neighbors are having."

The neighboring mansion was owned by Birdman, CEO of Cash Money Records. Alexus could only imagine what kind of party he was having.

"And Flako just called," Enrique said as the elevator began its descent.

"Yeah? What'd he want?"

"He was making sure you were okay. Told me to tell you that he's available if you need him to fly in. He's down in Bogota for a meeting with the Medellin and North Valley bosses. They're trying to raise the prices again."

"Uncle Flako can have that stupid cartel."

"Don't say that."

"Why not? I mean it. I am done."

"You're just upset. Vida left everything to you for a reason, Alexus. She saw in you what you did not see in yourself. She saw the strength. Papi saw it, too. That's why he groomed *you* to be the boss. You can't abandon the Costilla Family business. You were born to be the queen of the cartel. Vida always said you'd be the next boss. I bet if she—"

Enrique went silent abruptly.

They had just made it to the ground floor, and the doors were opening.

Special Agent Josh Sneed was standing just outside the elevator.

Chapter 30

Alexus stepped out of the elevator, pinched the bridge of her nose between her thumb and forefinger, closed her eyes, and gritted her teeth.

"What the hell do you want?" she asked.

"We need to talk."

"I just talked to those other FBI agents."

"Now you need to talk to me," Sneed said.

There were four FBI agents behind him. He glanced back at them and told them to head on out. He wouldn't be long.

Reluctantly, Alexus led him out to the rear patio deck where Mercedes was seated on a white leather sofa, gazing vacantly at the steaming cup of tea she had cradled in her hands. Alexus sat sown next to her grieving sister. Sneed stood before them with his arms crossed over his chest.

"Alexus Costilla," he said bitterly.

She hugged Mercedes and said nothing.

"I'm finally beginning to understand your role in all of this," Sneed said. "Back when you first inherited Costilla Corp., and your aunt, Jennifer, started her vicious attacks on you and your family, the Bureau concluded that she was merely angered by the fact that she'd been excluded from Vida Costilla's fifty-billion-dollar will. But it goes much deeper than that, doesn't it?"

"Don't be delusional," Alexus said.

"Delusional? You think I'm being delusional?" Palpable disbelief laced his tone. "I don't think so, Alexus. Ever heard of the Matamoros drug cartel? I'm quite sure you have. Your father was the leader."

"I don't know what you're talking about."

"You're the boss now, aren't you?"

"Of Costilla Crop.?"

"Don't play dumb with me."

"I'm not playing dumb. There are two CEOs of Costilla Crop., and I'm one of them. So yeah, I guess you can say I'm the boss now, but not of any drug cartel. I couldn't tell you the first thing about dealing drugs."

"You're lying to me, Alexus, lying through your pretty little teeth. But you know something?" Sneed's hands went to his hips and he waited.

"I don't know anything." Deny, Deny, Deny. Those had been Papi's three rules to dealing with federal authorities, and Alexus was sticking to them.

"I've finally gotten it through my head that the Costilla family is invincible in South America, Central America, and even here in North America. The level of corruption is unprecedented. I'm guessing you family has done things for the U.S. government that they simply cannot let get out to the public. *That's* why your father and his brother Flako were released from federal prison, and why I can't get a warrant signed against either of you. It has to be the reason. Well, you know what? I'm done trying. I just want your aunt brought to justice. I couldn't care less what happened after that."

Alexus didn't know how to respond to Sneed's dead-on accusations, so she flicked her eyes over to the private dock where her seventy-foot yacht was anchored.

"We almost had her," Sneed continued. "I think she slipped away after the car bombing, probably detonated it when she saw that my men were knocking on doors in your sister neighborhood. A guy who lived next door to Mercedes was found dead and decapitated. We're pretty sure it's Jenny's work."

"Just make sure you kill her if you catch her," Alexus said, rubbing a hand in circles on her distraught sibling's shoulder.

"Oh, she most certainly is going to be killed. She won't make it out of Chicago. We've got men everywhere." Sneed turned and gazed out over the ocean. Seconds later, he said, "I, uh… need a favor… if you can spare it, that is."

Alexus looked at him and frowned.

"Just forty grand," he said, "to get my restaurant up and running. I'd pay it back with interest."

"Write down your address. I'll have it delivered tomorrow."

"Has to be cash."

"It'll be cash."

"Thank you so much," he said. He took a small notepad and an ink pen out of his breast pocket, hesitated, and then wrote.

Alexus continued staring across the Olympic-sized swimming pool to the ocean beyond. Her two chefs were toiling over stainless steel grills ten feet behind Sneed, leaving the air heavily redolent of crab and shrimp and whatever else they were cooking. Enrique and a dozen more armed bodyguards in dark Hartmarx suits stood along the mansion's glass exterior walls.

Handing the paper bearing a Des Plaines, Illinois address to Alexus, Sneed said, "I'll have the loan returned by—"

"Don't worry about paying it back," Alexus interrupted. "Pay it forward. But remember, a favor done is a favor owned. Enrique will see you to the door."

"This can't get out."

"It won't."

"We're sending a look-alike to your father's old yacht on Sunday. Team Six will be in the water. If Jenny somehow makes it out of Chicago and to that boat in Malibu, we'll get her."

And with that he turned and left.

A part of Alexus wanted to berate Mercedes for letting the FBI agent know what Aunt Jenny had said on the phone, but Mercedes appeared far to hopeless and despondent. The scolding would have to wait.

The two sisters sat in silence for half an hour. Enrique went to bed. The chefs brought over plates of culinary masterpieces. Mercedes bit into a crab cake.

"I didn't think you'd eat anything," Alexus said, breaking the euphonious silence."

"She murdered my children," Mercedes murmured. "Cut off their heads."

"She's a sick woman."

"What kind of person murders innocent little kids?"

"A sick one."

"But she's our *aunt*." Mercedes started bawling. "We have the same last name as her, the same bloodline."

"We'll get even with her soon enough. What matters now is that we stay strong and fight back. We can do this, Mercedes. I see happiness at the end of the road, and we are going to get there. Together. I know we will."

Mercedes bawled for several minutes. Then Alexus sent the butler to fetch a bottle of Patron and two shot glasses. She talked to Mercedes into calming down and taking a shot with her. One shot turned into five, and soon they were thoroughly inebriated.

"You said one shot," Mercedes said.

"You're the one who poured the second shot," Alexus reminded.

"Yeah, and you poured the next thousand."

"We needed it."

"Well, now I'm drunk."

"You and me both," Alexus said.

Mercedes got up and wobbled on her Louboutin heels. "I'm going to bed, and I'm going to sleep like a bear."

"I just might pass out right here."

"Bitch, you better get upstairs in that bed. Don't forget we're in Miami. They got snakes and all kinda shit."

"I'll be fine," Alexus said. "Go to bed. I've got a plan brewing up in my head that'll be ready for presentation by morning. You'll like it."

She signaled for a bodyguard to escort Mercedes to a guest bedroom, then went to one of the lounge chairs next to the pool and reclined in it. She sent for another drink—an apple Ciroc martini—and stared up at the stars until it came.

Nursing the martini through a straw, Alexus trapped into her smartphone's photo gallery and flipped through her *Hubby* album. She had photos of Blake doing everything from sleeping to lifting weights; recording in the studio and preforming live on stage in stadiums all across the globe to play-fighting with King Neal and horseback riding with Savaria.

Then Alexus went to the video gallery.

There were seventy videos, but she was only interested in watching the five long recordings of her and Blake having sex. Each of them had been recorded with him holding the iPhone5. In the first video, Blake sat in a swivel chair with his pants and boxers around his ankles in the recording studio at the Highland Park mansion he'd bought from Michael Jordan. For fifteen minutes and twenty seconds, Alexus sucked and slurped and deep throated his lengthy ebony phallus in and out of her mouth. It ended with him striping her tongue with ribbons of cum.

The second video was similar, only Blake was lying on a bed aboard the Omnipotent, and instead of filling her mouth with semen he roped it across her face. The last three videos amounted to two hundred and forty-nine minutes of him fucking her missionary and doggy-style and her riding him cowgirl and reverse cowgirl on the same bed that was in the second video.

Observing herself riding and sucking him set Alexus in fire. Her pussy was wet. Her nipples were taut. She knew her bodyguards were keeping a close eye on her, but that didn't restrain her from lifting her short white dress, closing her eyes, and pushing her figure into her damp vaginal tunnel. She alternated between fingering herself and massaging her clitoris.

When Alexus open her eyes, she could not *believe* her eyes.

Standing to the right of her lounge chair was Porsche, to the left of the chair stood a shirtless Trey Songz, and filing out the patio door was a long line of Hip-Hop celebrities.

Alexus let out an embarrassed gasp and yanked down her dress.

"Ugh, Alexus, yo' lil nasty ass," Porsche said with a snicker as she grabbed her hips. "Everybody wanted to come over to show support for you and Rita, and Bulletface. Where's my sister? That bitch sleep already?"

"Yeah, she went to bed a little while ago," Alexus said, unable to take her eyes off of Trey's handsome brown face. He was smiling a Colgate smile and extending a hand to her for a shake. She laid her hand in his and melted, then pulled it back a second later when she thought of the dampness on her figures. "Oh, my—I'm so sorry. This is so embarrassing."

"No need to be embarrassed about that. It's a good thing," Trey said.

"Oh, my God, I *love* your music."

He chuckled. "Thanks."

Alexus glanced to her left again and saw that most of the YMCMB family—Tunechi, Drake, Nicki, Birdman, Tyga, DJ Khaled, and Busta—were among the visitors, as well as numerous bikini-clad models, Rick Ross and his MMB team, French Montana and his Coke Boyz artists, and Chyna who'd brought along eight of her fellow dancers from King of Diamonds.

Turing back to Trey, Alexus looked him up and down.

One little fling before I get married won't hurt, she thought.

Chapter 31

"How much did it cost you to bulletproof that Phantom?" Tahiry asked.

"Extra seventy bands," Blake said.

"Thank God you had it done. He could've killed me."

"Yeah, I know."

"French Montana must've made it to Miami already. He posted a pic on IG of everybody at Birdman's party. You should call Alexus and to tell her about the shooting. Don't let her find out from someone else."

Blake grinned and shook his head. He had watched Chief Keef and the Glory Boyz gang shoot up his Rolls Royce before dipping back into the Benz and racing away. Saved by the Phantom's bullet-resistant exterior, Blake had cut the trip to his Park Avenue apartment and decided instead to board his Gulfstream jet and fly straight to Chicago with Will Scrill and his goons in tow, leaving Tahiry in New York.

His private jet had landed at O'Hare ten minutes prior, and now he was leaving the airport in the backseat of his matte black four-door Bugatti

Galibier. Young Meach was driving. Scrill was next to Blake, and P.A.T., whose arm was in a sling to support his wounded shoulder, was in the passenger seat beside Meach.

Blake was FaceTiming with Tahiry on his iPhone5.

"I'll talk to Alexus in the mornin'. I gotta go," Blake said.

"Be safe out there."

"I'll be good."

"Don't do anything crazy."

"I won't."

"Promise?" she asked.

Blake grinned and hung up. He looked back at the second black Galibier that was following the one he was in. It was occupied by Cup, Lil Cholly, and two more TVLs from Chicago's Lawndale neighborhood, and the three black Escalades behind it were filled with gun-toting Vice Lords and Four Corner Hustler gang members.

It was just two minutes past midnight in Chicago, and Blake knew that Chicago always became Chiraq on warm summer nights like this.

The Mac-11 submachine gun on his lap had a fifty-round clip. He was more than ready to empty it.

"So," Meach asked, "the nigga just pulled up and started dumpin'? The fuck was he doin' in New York?"

"Frenchy say the nigga was recordin' some shit wit' Lady Gaga," Blake said, sipping from his Styrofoam cup of Lean. "I was in the backseat wit' Tahiry when he hopped out and started shootin' my window. Tadoe was blowin' too. Tahiry got to screamin' and shit, but I knew it was bulletproof so I just stared at 'em till they pulled off."

"You fuck Tahiry?" Meach asked.

"Man," Scrill said, "he had her, I had K. Michelle, and we didn't fuck either one of them."

"That's fucked up," P.A.T. commented.

"On Angelo," Meach added.

"All dat ass," Scrill said, shaking his bald brown head.

Glancing at Blake in the rearview mirror, Meach said, "Why would you wanna fuck Tahiry when you got Alexus? She got just as much ass as

Tahiry and just as bad. You trippin', bruh. On Chief Lo."

"I ain't trippin', nigga. Just get me to O-Block so I can kill somebody."

"Awready." Meach turned up the volume on BulletFace's "Shoot Em Down" and put fire to the end of a blunt.

'My nigga Meachie called me said we got another problem
I went and got my choppa call dat bitch my problem solver
Swear we got everything from AKs straight down to revolvers
And bitch we hold court in the streets, my K got fifty lawyers
I'll do it now... pull up on some fuck niggas and shoot em down
Ringlin' Brothers wit' these choppas nigga all we do is clown
No new friends lil nigga don't make me treat you like you new in town
Bitch I'll bring out all my hammers and nail all yo' shooters down...'

Blake hit the blunt when it made it around to him, then passed it forward to Meach.

"We found out where dat nigga Ant live," Scrill said, leaning toward Blake so his voice could be heard over the music.

"Yeah?" Sounded like good news to Blake.

"Yep. Thirty-Fifth and Madison in Gary. I think it's his brother's house."

"We on that."

"Want me to send Rube to handle dat now? I'll throw him twenty racks for the hit."

"Nah," Blake said. "I wanna do it myself. We'll slide out there later."

"You really shouldn't be puttin' yo'self on the front line like dat, Lord. Put dat bankroll to work."

"Fuck that."

"Don't be hard-headed."

"Fuck that," Blake repeated. He took a big gulp of Lean.

Will Scrill left it alone.

Lowering the music volume, Meach said, "Call Lakita, bruh. She know some niggas out of Englewood. See if she can lead us to em."

Blake considered it a good idea, so he phoned Lakita Thomas, the ex of his who'd given him the warning at the service station last night. She didn't answer the first time he called. He waited a couple of seconds and called back. Kita picked up after the third ring.

"Hey, boy," she said cheerfully.

"Where you at?"

"Leaving Arnie's wit' my girl Shay. Why?"

"I need your help."

She sucked her teeth. "What now?"

"You know where to find any of Chief Keef's people."

"Oh, Lord."

"I got a hun'ed racks for you…"

"I don't do that shit no more, Blake. And even if I did, it wouldn't be to them GBE nigga. They're the ones killing everybody out there on the south side."

Blake swallowed a mouthful of Lean. "That's fucked up," he said.

"What's fucked up?" she asked. "That I won't set somebody up for you?"

"It's cool."

"Don't do this me, Blake. Those guys will kill me if—"

"*Two* hun'ed racks."

Kita sighed.

Blake sipped and waited.

"Okay, listen," Kita said finally. "I just saw Tray Savage makin' it rain on some bitches at Arnie's. He's GBE. He left out right before I did. He wants to fuck but I've been dodging him. I got his number. Pretty sure I can get him to meet you somewhere. But I'm telling you now, if this shit goes wrong, I'm cussing you out. I have a daughter, Blake."

"I understand that. I got a daughter, too."

"Yeah, but you can protect her with all those millions. I'm not a millionaire like you."

"I'll make sure you and your daughter are safe."

"You better."

"I most definitely will," Blake said, accepting a freshly rolled blunt from Scrill. "Just tell me where to find that nigga."

"I'm about to call and see if he can meet me at this gas station I just pulled into. It's the Citgo on 116th and Michigan."

"Call him on three-way."

"Okay, mute your phone," Kita said. "And Shay wants in, too."

"I got both of y'all," Blake said.

Chapter 32

Alexus wondered if Trey Songz knew how wet her pussy was getting simply from the feel of his hands on her right foot.

She'd reeled him in with a wince and a rub of the ankle mere seconds after she opened her eyes to find him and Porsche at the lower end of her lounge chair. That was fifteen minutes ago, and he was still massaging her ankle and foot.

Alexus Costilla was in heaven.

"You are so good with those hands of yours," she said softly.

Nicki Minaj was sitting up in the lounge chair to Alexus's left, and Blac Chyna was reclined in the one to the right of Alexus. Most of the girls who came with them were in the swimming pool with Wale and Lil Durk, and the others were mingling with the rap gods on the other side of the pool.

"Girl," Nicki said, "he wanna do you just as bad as you wanna do him. Am I right Trey?"

Alexus blushed.

Trey Songz chuckled and said nothing.

Chyna said, "Every woman in the world would be so jealous of you if they knew who was rubbing your foot right now. I know I am."

"Don't get me wrong," Nicki said, swatting at a mosquito, "Bulletface is fine as hell, but damn, Trey. You got *me* all worked up over here. Think I might need a massage when you get done with her. I got something you can massage."

Alexus rolled her eyes, smiling uncontrollably. She sent the butler off for more drinks and to grab one of the white leather Chanel suitcases out of her bedroom.

"Thank you so much, you're such a sweetheart," Alexus said as she sat up and grabbed her heels from beside her lounge chair. She was trying her best to keep from pouncing on Trey, so she focused on putting on the heels as he stood in front of her, his perfect brown abdomen lurking less than a foot from her forehead.

Her vaginal muscles quivered.

"See now," Nicki said, "I wouldn't be able to take that."

"Mmm mmm *mmm,*" Chyna added.

Rolling her eyes again, Alexus got up, placed her hands on her hips, and flicked her eyes from Chyna to Nicki and back to Chyna. "You two bitches need to stop instigating. Y'all know I'm with Blake, and I'm sure Trey has a lucky young lady of his own."

"Umm, actually he doesn't," Chyna said.

Trey put his arm around Alexus' shoulders and hugged her close against his side. She felt her heartbeats double in speed.

"I'm saving myself for you, Alexus," he said.

Alexus nearly fainted. The drinks and her suitcase arrived, and she had to peel away from her favorite singer to get a little more Ciroc in her system. Then she opened the suitcase.

The eyes of her guests went wide.

Inside the suitcase was five million dollars in bank-new hundreds.

"Chyna, I would really appreciate it if you taught me a few of those stripper tricks," Alexus said, lifting several ten-thousand-dollar bundles out of the suitcase. "Better yet, let's have a twerk contest! A hundred thousand to the winner."

This grabbed the girls' attention. Those in the swimming pool clambered out hurriedly. Alexus tore of the paper money bands and got ready to make it rain—anything to keep her mind off of Trey Songz.

His cologne was in her nostrils. She still felt the warmth of his arm on her shoulders, though it was no longer there. She wondered how many inches he was packing, and if he'd utilize every inch if she gave him the opportunity.

Stop thinking about fucking this guy, she thought to herself as she swiped crisp Benjamins at Chyna's undulant butt cheeks. Within minutes, she had $80,000 scattered across the smooth white marble next to the pool.

Then French Montana walked up beside Alexus and said something that made her forget all about Trey Songz.

"Fucked up how they shot up ya man's Phantom after the show. Lucky that muhfucka was bullet-proof."

Alexus handed the cash in her hands to French and went for her smartphone.

Chapter 33

"They just pulled up in a green Tahoe. Shit, he brought two other guys. Make sure you don't shoot me and Shay. Please."

Blake ended the call and stared across the street at the Tahoe. He was sitting in the backseat of one of his black-on-black Escalades with the Mac-11 embraced firmly in his right hand. The guys who'd been in the Escalade before were now in his Bugatti with P.A.T, and with him in the Escalade were Meach, Scrill, and Rube.

"Drive over there, nigga! Catch 'em before they get out," Rube said, chambering a round in his AK-47.

Meach said, "That gas station got cameras. Let's just run over—"

"Come on," Blake said, pushing open his door.

Sprinting across the street, he raised the Mac-11 and was about to unload on the Tahoe's driver's door when the door behind it opened and a young guy with dreadlocks stepped out. Blake took aim at him and sent a spray of bullets into his chest. Rube appeared beside him and started firing on the Tahoe as its driver accelerated out of the gas station, while Blake ran up on the boy he'd shot and spayed him again, this time in the face. Then he turned and—like Meach, Scrill, and Rube—squeezed off shots at the escaping Tahoe until it crashed into a parked Ford pickup on 177th.

The driver leapt out, bravely returning fire, and so did the passenger. Long clips hung from the bottoms of their handguns. They attempted to flee in separate directions, but the passenger was cut down by Meach's chrome-plated Tec-9.

Blake spotted Kita and Shay crouching down next to an Impala at the Citgo. They seemed okay. He and his guys were back in the Escalade and speeding off seconds later.

The Bugattis and the other two Escalades were parked in an alley five blocks down. Blake didn't speak until he was seated behind the driver's seat of his Galibier; Alexus was in his missed calls, and he loved her too much to wait even a second to return the call. They went straight to FaceTime.

"Somebody shot at you in New York?" she asked immediately.

"Love you, baby." He grinned at her perfectly-sculpted biracial visage.

"Don't fuck with me, Blake."

"Who told you about it?"

"Frenchy's here. Porsche went next door to Birdman's place and brought back his whole party. But talk me about the shooting. Who did it?"

"Same nigga we saw wit' the K last night, the one I let get way."

"Why didn't you call and tell me about this? You could've been killed, Blake. Jesus Christ."

"I'm Louis, baby. Don't worry about me. I got me." He slid the Mac under Meach's seat as the Bugatti lurched out of the alley. Studying his lady's face on the iPhone5 screen, he said, "I should've just flown to Miami."

"You in Chicago?"

"Yup."

"Good. Have somebody put a hundred bullets in every house on his block."

"I'm already on it."

"God, I am so horny. I wish you'd have flown here first."

"I know, baby." He glimpsed Trey Songz and Lil Wayne in the background behind Alexus and frowned. "Fuck are y'all doin'?"

"Twerk contest."

"Wit' who?"

"Chyna and some other bitches from K.O.D."

"Don't get fucked up."

"I'm not involved."

"Like I said," Blake repeated, "don't get fucked up."

"All I'm doing is throwing money. Relax."

"Nah, fuck all dat. What the fuck—I just saw Trey Songz standin' behind you."

"They were at Birdman's party. They came over with Porsche. I just told you that."

"Vari asleep?"

"Both of them are."

"Is Mercedes there?"

"Yeah. She just went to bed not too long ago. We took a bunch of shots of Patron, and she loosened up a bit."

"Glad she's alright," Blake said, glancing out his back window at Cup's identical Bugatti. "I just had a talk wit' one of Keef's guys. On my way out west wit' Cup now."

"I don't trust him," Alexus said.

"No shit, Sherlock."

"I wanted him dead when I shot him."

"Of course you did. Why else would you shoot him?"

"Just… be careful. Don't let that gang shit get in the way of you remembering who kidnapped your daughter and slit her mother's throat."

"I'll never forget that."

"Well, I'm just saying…"

Blake heard sirens in the distance. Meach was zipping the Galibier down Michigan, and soon they were out of the "Wild Hundreds."

He said, "I'm postin' on Twitter soon's we get to 15th and Trumbull, just to let niggas know where I'm at. That way, Chief Keef, T-Walk, *and* Jenny can find me if they want to. I ain't duckin' nobody."

"Whatever you do, be smart, Blake. Think things through. As long as you and I are on the winning end of things, we'll be good. But we have to win. Every single time, we have to win."

"You just make sure you stay the fuck away from Trey Songz. I know how much you like that nigga."

"Boy," Alexus said, smiling guiltily.

"A'ight," Blake warned. "You saw how my nigga Tip was at Floyd."

"So what? It's not like I'd get hurt."

"I'll fuck you up, too."

"You ain't gon' do shit."

Blake smiled at Alexus, and she smiled back. He heard French Montana's timeless club banger "Pop That" booming through the smartphone. Glancing at his diamond watch, he saw that it was almost 1:00 A.M.

"I'll be at you tomorrow, baby," he said. "Take your ass to bed and go to sleep. Don't make me fuck you up."

"My pussy's dripping wet."

"I'll be home by sunrise."

"You'd better be. I'm telling you now, I'd be fucking Trey Songz brain's out if not for you."

Blake's brows furrowed. "What?!" He was incredulous.

"I was only kidding."

"No the fuck you—"

"I was joking, Blake—"

"Fuck that. Fly out here *tonight*. Right now. I wanna see you all the way to the airport."

"You think I'd actually cheat on you?"

"I don't know. I could've fucked Tahiry today. I *should've* fucked Tahiry today."

Alexus scowled at him. "I'll kill your ass."

"Well," Blake said, taking has first sip of Lean since he'd gotten out of the Escalade, "stay the fuck away from niggas you wanna fuck, and I'll stay the fuck away from bitches I wanna fuck."

"You're right."

"I know I'm right."

"Shut up."

"Why I need to shut up?" Blake asked. He accepted a blunt from Scrill, while thumbing through the new text messages on his other iPhone5 from Lakita. There were two of them:

'Savage just sent me a text saying I'm dead,' the first text read.

'HE JUST CALLED!' read the second.

"You're right," Alexus said. "I'm about to pay these girls for their twerking skills and send them home."

"I really could've fucked Tahiry."

"I'll kill you and that bitch. Cut off both your heads."

"Yeah, a'ight," Blake smirked arrogantly.

"I'm serious, Blake."

"I am, too. I want you in the bed wit' me when I go to sleep tonight. And you better—never mind. Just get here."

"You're the one who's supposed to be here with me. I could've gotten my brains blown out at the Versace mansion tonight. And that damned psychotherapist told my mom *every*thing about me, so now my mom's mad. I called Miller. He said she's praying at some church here in Miami. I swear, sometimes I think she's *too* religious."

"Vari and King okay?"

"Yeah. They're sleeping."

Blake held his breath as a CPD squad car sped past with its lights flashing and its siren blaring. His second smartphone began ringing with a call from Lakita. He ignored the call, glanced at his icy watch, and sipped some Lean.

Alexus said, "I'm drunk."

"Well, take your ass to bed."

"I'm about to now. You flying back tonight or in the morning?"

"In the morning."

"Okay. Be careful out there. Love you."

"Love you, too," he said.

Blake tried to relax. He thought long and hard and ultimately decided it was best to keep up his attacks on the Glory Boyz gang, especially since T-Walk was posting pics on Instagram with Chief Keef… at *Cup's* nightclub.

He picked up the second iPhone5 to dial Cup's number but Kita called back before he could make it to Cup. Reluctantly, he answered.

Kita spoke frantically.

"They're gonna kill me, Blake. He keeps calling. Everybody knows I dance at—"

"Calm the fuck down."

"How am I supposed to calm down? This nigga won't stop calling my phone! He's calling me again now."

"Where you at?"

"93rd and Michigan."

"I'm on 79th and Michigan." He told Meach to pull over. "Hurry up. We'll wait on you, and then you can follow us out west, to 15th and Trumbull. I got that bread in my truck. You can stay wit' me all night, and I promise, by noon I'll have you and Shay in a twenty-million-dollar condo in whatever city y'all choose."

"I want us both on a plane by sunrise, Blake. Please don't get us get killed out here in these streets."

"You'll be safe wit' me. I'm the *king* of these streets. Just chill the fuck out and come on."

He ended the call. Meach had pulled over seconds ago, and there was a steatopygic redbone in small denim shorts standing on the corner that had everybody's attention. She and her four friends— one male and three females—looked to be in their early twenties.

All their eyes were unwaveringly glued to the two black Bugattis as Cup's pulled up alongside Blake's.

Blake rolled down his window.

Meach said, "Y'all see how thick this bitch on the corner is? Gotdamn she strapped, on Lo."

Cup's window came down, and his bald brown head poked out of it. Like Blake, he had his head stashed deep in a black-and-gold Versace hoody and there was a heavy gold and diamond chain draping from his neck.

"The fuck we stoppin' for?" Cup asked.

Blake answered the question with a question. "What was up wit' Chief Keef and T-Walk at the Visionary Lounge last night? That was right before they came through dumpin' on me and my niggas. You *know*. I'm blowin' about that, *and* about my nigga Yellow gettin' murked."

"Man, I ain't got nothin' to do wit' that shit. That nigga just spent eight milli with *me,* so evidently me and T-Walk are on *great* terms. And Chief Keef's my lil guy. I've never talked to him, but he comes to my clubs, blows through racks on bottles and food with his crew, showers my dancers in thousands, then *I* get a cut out of every night. As long as I continue to allow him and his gang in with their guns, they're gonna keep blowing money at my establishments. It'd be a dumb move business-wise to go against Chief Keef or T-Walk. But look, we can talk about this shit when we make it back to the block. Why y'all pull over?"

"Waitin' on ol' girl. Bubbles."

"My stripper Bubbles?"

"Yup."

"Man, she is stupid-thick. I love that girl. Never fucked her, but I most definitely would. I still remember when she first started danc—"

Cup was silenced by a sudden screech of tires.

A dark-colored Buick SUV had just rushed to a stop on the corner of 79th and Michigan. The

driver—a dark-skinned teen with dreadlocks—
jumped out, aiming a pistol with a frighteningly
long clip at the guy on the corner with the four girls.

There was a deadly boom and a hellacious
flash.

The four girls froze as the innards of their
friend's skull left the back of his head in a
gelatinous crimson mist.

Then the SUV disappeared down 79th Street.

Chapter 34

Alexus knew she'd had too much to drink.

She was wobbling on her diamond-encrusted heels with her jaw resting on Nicki's shoulder, lazily nodding her head to the beat of French Montana's "Pop That" as it played from behind the fully-stocked beverage bar across the pool. She'd decided to give all twelve girls who participated, in the impromptu twerk-a-thon $100,000 apiece; Porsche was handing out the hefty cash bundles, while the ladies who hadn't participated scooped up hundreds of crisp Benjamins from the smooth marble ground.

"You need to take your butt to bed," Chyna said.

"Don't throw up on my shoulder," Nicki warned.

"Help me up to—tell one of the bodyguards to carry me," Alexus said in a half slur. She closed her eyes and tried to stop the world from spinning out of control.

Suddenly, she was lifted into a pair of strong arms and carried away, but she was far too intoxicated to open her eyes and see whose arms they were. She heard the *ding* of the elevator, heard

Porsche confabulating with two bodyguards. Her eyes popped open as the arms laid her out on her bed's soft white blanket.

The arms belonged to Trey Songz.

He was smiling down at Alexus, his expression as magical and stunning as that of an angel's. Porsche was wheeling the Chanel suitcase into the massive walk-in closet, and there were two bodyguards flanking the ajar bedroom door.

Alexus could not take her eyes off of the handsome young singer.

"Sweet dreams, beautiful," he said.

"Oh, my God," Alexus exclaimed. "You are, like, the finest man on the planet. It doesn't get much better than you and August Alsina."

"Trust me, we're both just as attracted to you. He and I were just talking about you at the BET awards sound check. He said you remind him of Mizz DR. You know who that is?"

"I know I want you to kiss me."

He chuckled. "You know I can't do that, Alexus, no matter how badly I want to—which I assure you I do."

"Why not?"

"Because you're with Bulletface."

"And?" she persisted. "He fucked Rihanna and I took him back. If he feels it's okay to fuck her then I feel it's okay for me to fuck you."

"Two wrongs don't make a right."

"Great sex makes *every*thing right."

"Yeah. I suppose. But sex ain't better than love." Trey showed an even broader smile, apparently amused with himself over his play of words. "I'm telling you, your relationship with Bulletface is gonna be like Beyoncé and Jay, but it won't happen until you two see what y'all have in each other. Remember that, and thank me later."

He pulled her hand to his lip, kissed the back of it, then turned and left the bedroom just as Porsche emerged from the closet looking just as drunk-faced as Alexus.

Beaming merrily, Alexus flung herself about the bed in an overly exaggerate tantrum.

Porsche cracked up laughing.

"Bitch, you just had Trey Songz in your bedroom," Porsche said.

"Don't remind me."

"I'm sorry, but my man would've had to fuck me up over this one. I'd divorce a husband on a honeymoon for some of Trey Songz."

"And you think I wouldn't?"

"You sure didn't try. Or at least not as hard as I would've tried. I would've been asshole-naked up in here." Porsche laughed heartily. "Had the chance of a lifetime, and you blew it."

"I'm surprised I didn't have an orgasm when he was massaging my foot."

"I'm surprised you didn't climb on top of him and ride him until *he* had an orgasm. Lord knows I would've."

They laughed together... until Alexus felt the acidic burn of bile rising in her throat.

She dashed to the bathroom and managed to kneel in front of the toilet a millisecond before the vomit came exploding out of her mouth. She flinched awkwardly as Porsche began rubbing her back.

"Relax, girl. It's only me," Porsche said soothingly.

"I swear to"—more vomit gushed out of her and landed thickly in the toilet water—"God, I'm never drinking again."

"Sure, sure. That's what we all say."

"I'm serious."

"I know you are. Maybe next time you'll be sober enough to take full advantage when Trey Songz carries you to bed."

"Shut up." Alexus laughed and wiped her eyes and heaved twice more. "Ugh, this is so disgusting."

"You're a rookie. Can't hold your liquor."

"I'm just not an alcoholic like *some* people."

"Like who?"

"I'm not saying any names. If the shoe fit, paint the bottom of that motherfucker red and rock that shit."

Again they laughed. Alexus wiped her mouth, flushed the frothy vomit, sighed, and shook her head ashamedly as she scooted to the wall and rested her back against it. She buried her face in her hands and let out a second sigh. Then a third.

"Damn, you are fucked up," Porsche said. "Want me to run you some bathwater?"

"Please do. I'd really appreciate it."

"No problem." Porsche sat on the side of the vintage cabriole-legged tub and started the water. "It's okay to turn up a little every now and then, but don't drink to cover up the pain. You'll only feel worse afterward."

"I know."

"I'm just as sad as you are, Alexus, if not sadder. I loved my niece and nephew to pieces. Jenny Costilla is a monster. There is a special place in hell for people like her, you know that?"

"I'm sure there is."

"Takes a sick motherfucker to kill a kid."

"Jenny's way past sick. I'm hoping they can catch her and kill her before she can kill again."

A brief silence followed. The cool feel of glass on her cheek reminded Alexus that she was still holding her smartphone. She dropped her head back and stared at it.

"Hey," Porsche asked, "Do you always give away money like you did tonight. That was over a million dollars you had me pass out."

"My cartel makes me about nine hundred million tax free dollars every month. I can afford to splurge a little."

"Shit, you're rich."

"It's not as fun as you think it is. The damned cartel makes it all too dangerous. That and Blake's crazy ass."

Porsche's dark-skinned face lit up. "A'ight now, bitch, you know how much I love me some Bulletface. He cain't do no wrong in my book."

"Oh, please."

"Stop hatin', Bulletface is the shit, and you know it. He's the best rapper ever. Name another nigga who can rap better than him."

"I never said he wasn't a great lyricist, but…"

"I don't wanna hear it. You're a hater," Porsche said. "And hatin' on your own man, too. That's a damned shame."

"Whatever." Alexus moved to her knees, put her smartphone on the floor, took off her clothes and jewelry, and climbed into the tub.

The water was almost scalding-hot.

"Cold, cold, cold," Alexus said quickly, and Porsche immediately turned off the cold water. "I meant *add* cold water," she shrieked, squinting at the unbearable heat and leaping out of the tub.

"Oh, shit," Porsche said with a devious snicker. "My bad."

"You bitch."

"Sorry sis. I honestly did not mean to do that."

"How could you *accidentally* have the water that hot? That was deliberate Porsche." Scowling, Alexus walked naked to the stainless steel sink, snatched open the top drawer, and hoisted out an ominously heavy gold-plated .50-caliber Desert Eagle with a golden 50-round drum magazine underneath its handle and red laser sighting on top of its barrel.

Alexus put the red dot on the tip of Porsche's aquiline nose.

"What the fuck?" Porsche exclaimed.

"You burned me on purpose," Alexus accused.

"Do you really think I'd do something like that?"

"I don't know. Would you?" Alexus kept the gun on Porsche for an uncomfortably long ten seconds. Then she lowered it slowly, laughed once, and stepped back into the tub. "Just kidding."

"No you weren't. That was the crazy Mexican cartel boss in you."

Settling into the warm soapy water, Alexus noticed the room wasn't spinning as wildly as it had been moments earlier. The throwing up had helped. Her mental balance was returning.

She smiled at Porsche.

"You're nuts, Alexus."

"Just don't burn me again."

Chapter 35

Trumbull Avenue was jam packed from 16th Street to Douglas Boulevard. Parked along the street were two black Rolls-Royce Phantoms, three black Bugatti Veyrons, and more older-model Chevys and Oldsmobiles on big chrome rims than one could count on four hands, so Meach was forced to park in the dark alley, followed by Cup's identical Galibier and Shay's burgundy Impala.

Getting out of the two-million-dollar sedan, Blake flared his nostrils and inhaled the savory aroma of grilled meats that filled the air. Cup's people were barbecuing on the corner of 15th and Trumbull, and a part of Blake wanted to head straight to the corner for a plate.

Another part of him wanted to erase the grotesque memory of the five bullet holes he'd left in the boy's face at Citgo.

He immediately walked over to Cup. "You say T-Walk spent some millions with you? Where he at?"

"I really don't know. Couldn't tell if I did," Cup said, already rolling a blunt of Kush. "Man, let that shit go and enjoy yourself. We got food, weed, and bitches out here, and we're the kings of the land. Let's blow this loud and blow some money."

Blake didn't reply. Instead, he turned and swaggered back to his car where his MBM gang was standing with Shay and Kita. The two girls were stunning in their snug-fitting mini-dresses and Louboutin heels. Shay was slender and modelesque. Kita was nearly as thickly-proportioned as Alexus.

Both of them looked scared out of their minds.

"Y'all wanna go eat?" Blake asked, sipping from his double Styrofoam.

"Hell no," Kita said. "What we wanna do is get the fuck out of Chicago."

"Exactly," Shay added.

"Scary asses," Blake said. He had Meach pop the trunk. Then he reached in it and lifted out a Louis Vuitton duffle bag.

Packed inside of it was $500,000 in hundred dollar bills.

"Here," he said, handing the duffle to Lakita "Bubbles" Thomas. "That's a half million. Have fun."

Scrill said, "Face, we need to go and tend to that situation in the G. We can demonstrate that thought and be right back on the jet."

Blake nodded. He was staring at Shay and Kita as they gawked into the cash-filled duffle bag. He contemplated posting his location on Twitter and Instagram in hopes of luring his enemies to the area, but it didn't seem like a bright idea. Not with Cup associating with both T-Walk and Chief Keef.

Thank God for the invention of bulletproof vests. Blake wore one under his Versace hoody, and the clip to the Mac-11in his boxers was already refilled to its full 50-round capacity.

The three Bugatti Veyrons parked on Trumbull Avenue were Blake's, driven there by Shannon, Tooter, and Snottz, members of his Dub Life crew in his hometown of Michigan City, Indiana. Several of the blacked-out '77 Chevy Caprice convertibles on Trumbull had also arrived packed full of Dub Life members, young black men and women with pockets and purses full of cash.

Kita locked the duffle in Shay's trunk and said, "We'll stay with you until you get to the airport."

Blake was okay with that.

Aplomb, he started across the lot to Trumbull Avenue. Cup fell in step beside him, and everyone else followed.

"You and T-Walk really need to drop the beef, lil homie," Cup said. "You and Chief Keef, too. If it ain't about money it ain't about nuthin'. Let's get this bread, lil nigga. I'm tryna get filthy rich like you."

"We're good." Blake grinned widely. "I don't want war wit' nobody. I'm the only billionaire we got in the streets. *I'm* the king, nigga. Fuck these other niggas. If it ain't about *Bulletface,* it ain't about nothin'."

"Don't get too arrogant."

"Ain't no such thing." Blake sipped some Lean and pointed at a chocolate girl who was sitting on the hood of a box Chevy with a red plastic cup in her hand.

"Fuck is you pointin' at?" Cup asked.

"That's Ebanee. I took her to Miami Beach and fucked her brains out twice last year. Best pussy ever."

"Better than Alexus?"

"Nigga!" Blake snarled, turning to Cup. "Don't worry about Alexus! That's *my* bitch. *My* pussy."

Cup threw up his hands in surrender and laughed. "My bad, lil homie."

"I don't play about my bitch, nigga."

"I said my bad." Cup smiled. "You remind me so much of Lil Lord. Same angry-ass demeanor. Will shoot anybody."

"On King Neal."

Cup glanced over his shoulder at Kita. "You ever fucked Bubbles?"

"Gunfire pussy," Blake confirmed.

"I *know* it is. Damn, she's so thick. If I didn't have Roz, my wife, I would've cuffed Bubbles when I first met her."

Blake nodded his head in agreement. His eyes were everywhere at once, searching vigilantly for any signs of strong hostility or antagonism. There were none… that was, until he arrived at the sidewalk.

An SUV turned off of 16th and came barreling down Trumbull Avenue.

Blake drew his submachine gun just as the window behind the SUV's driver slid down and an assault rifle emerged from it.

Bulletface opened fire.

Chapter 36

T-Walk ordered his driver to stop at the corner of 16th and Trumbull.

From there, he watched the ensuing shootout.

"Oh, my God! Ashley yelped as she dove onto him in the backseat of his blue Mercedes Maybach.

T-Walk didn't flinch. "Watch, baby," he said.

"They're shooting!"

"I know. Just watch."

"I can't."

"Yes, you can. Sit up."

Slowly, hesitantly, Ashley "Thunder" Hunter raised her head.

Four men on the sidewalk halfway down Trumbull Avenue were shooting at their approaching attackers.

"That's Bulletface they're shooting at," T-Walk said.

"How do you know that?" Thunder asked.

"They wouldn't have started shooting."

"I hope they kill him this time."

"So do I," T-Walk said.

Thunder rose another few inches. "Daaaanm, they are shooting like crazy."

"They just need to shoot Blake."

"But what if they don't? What if they miss?"

"Then I'll try again," T-Walk said.

"This shit is getting out of hand."

"It's *what*?" T-Walk scoffed incredulously. "It's GD till the world blow up. Fuck these niggas."

Chapter 37

Twenty minutes later Blake, was smoking Kush in the backseat of his Galibier as Meach zoomed down the interstate en route to Indiana. Kita had somehow ended up next to Blake. Shay, Scrill, and P.A.T. were two car-lengths behind in the Impala.

"You must have the worst luck in the history of the world," Kita murmured tremulously. "It's like you attract bullets or somethin'."

"Niggas just be hatin'. It's all good," Blake said.

"I'm scared, Blake."

"I know. But ain't no need to be scared. I'll make sure you're safe."

"I thought we were going to the airport? Why are we on the highway?"

"Got some business to handle first."

"Another shooting?" she asked.

Blake grinned at her. "How's your daughter?"

"Answer me."

"What's her name again? Ra'Mya, right?"

"You're gonna get us all killed."

"We ain't dead yet," he pointed out.

"You've been shot fourteen times," she said. "I might not be so lucky."

"You'll be good."

"Why do you keep risking your life out here in these streets? You're rich. You, Chief Keef, T-Walk." She shook her head skeptically. "I'm done with this lifestyle. I've had enough. From now on, I'm staying the fuck away from Chicago, Gary, and any other city where all niggas wanna do is shoot each other. I'm takin' my baby to a small town somewhere in Florida. I'ma lay out in the sun all day while Ra'Maya's at school, maybe find me a husband."

Blake chuckled and went to Instagram on one of his smartphones.

"What's funny?" Kita asked. Suddenly, she was interested in her own iPhone5.

"Nothin'."

"It's gotta be somethin'."

He shrugged. "Everybody wanna get married. I don't see what's so special about it. I'm about to get married to Alexus, but I don't even really understand it. Why we need to get married? She's already my woman, you feel me?"

"Marriage is everything to a woman. We all want somebody who will stand by our side when nobody else will, somebody who'll pick us up when we fall, care for us when we're sick. Hold us when we need to be held. Any woman will tell you, there's nothing like having a shoulder to cry on and a big dick to ride on. Some bitches will even settle for a small dick if he's nice enough. You happen to have a gigantic dick and you know to fuck a bitch through the bed with it. I'd marry you, too."

He looked over at her and nudged an elbow into her shoulder. She was smirking at her smartphone. "I miss you, Kita, you know that? You and Nauti."

"You don't miss me," she said, then gasped; she was scrolling down her Facebook page. "Damn. It says here that"—she turned to him wearing a shocked expression—"four people were shot and killed in the 1500 block of South Trumbull Avenue."

It wasn't breaking news to Blake. While Kita and Shay had gone scrambling for cover, he'd run up on the gunmen's SUV and put bullets in their heads, though they'd already been critically wounded.

"That's, like, eight murders in twenty-four hours, Blake. You're doing too much. Stop putting yourself in crazy, fucked up situations. You do know you're not invincible, right? Keep this shit up and you'll be dead or in prison for the rest of your life. Is that what you want?"

Blake stared thoughtfully at a picture Kelly Rowland had just uploaded to Instagram, momentarily lost in contemplation.

"Is that what you want?" Kita repeated.

"I just wanna live," he said finally.

"Well, start acting like it."

Chapter 38

Alexus woke up at 9:00 the following morning to a wonderful surprise.

"Morning, baby," Blake said, smiling broadly.

He was standing next to the bed holding a gold tray. On it was a plate of breakfast—a meaty omelet, hash browns, and buttery grits—and a tall glass of cold milk. A single red rose lay beside the plate.

Alexus sat up, wiping her eyes and yawning lazily. She looked up at Blake as he placed the tray on her lap. He smelled like he'd just gotten out of the shower and sprayed on a dash of cologne. He wore no shirt, just baggy black Rock Revival jeans with a gold-buckled Louis Vuitton belt and black Louboutin sneakers. He put a hand on her shoulder and planted a kiss on her cheek.

"When'd you get in?" she asked.

"Couple hours ago, 'bout four o'clock."

"Jesus Christ. Did you get any sleep?"

"Yeah, I slept on the plane. Then I took a nap when I got here. I waited in bed with you until Varia woke me up at seven, cryin' about King peeing in the bed. Told her she should've been in her own damn bed."

Alexus laughed. "Hilarious."

"Too funny. I laughed my ass off, and the more I laughed the more she cried. They're downstairs playin' Monopoly with Tamera."

She forked a piece of omelet in her month, picked up the rose, and rolled it between her fingers. "What did you do in Chicago? And please don't tell me you got your own hands dirty."

"Okay. I won't tell you."

"Oh my God, Blake."

"I had to do it, baby. That nigga Sosa tried to kill me in New York last night. I couldn't let that shit slide."

"You could've paid somebody to do the dirty work."

"I did. I paid a bitch to set the nigga up, then I—"

"Wait a minute. What bitch?"

"Kita."

"Hmmm."

"I didn't fuck her or nothin', just paid her to set him up. She's actually the reason I changed my mind and came home to you instead of goin' to Gary to catch the nigga who shot up your limo."

"Really?" She said skeptically.

"I'm dead serious." Blake walked around to his side of the bed, kicked off his sneakers, and cuddled up next to Alexus. He kissed her on the temple. "We had a talk about relationships, and that street shit. I gotta fall back for King Neal and Vari, and for you. I'm done shootin' at these niggas. I'ma start puttin' money on their heads. My lil nigga can't wait to catch a body."

"How long have I been telling you that?" Alexus said as she picked up the TV remote from her nightstand and turned on the 80" flat-screen on the wall across from the bed. She went straight to MTN News—one of her own television networks—and gritted her teeth at the caption on the bottom of the screen:

BILLIONAIRE ALEXUS COSTILLA'S "VERSACE" MANSION ATTACKED BY GUNMEN; 18 DEAD

The words scrolling across beneath the caption read*: Rapper Yellowboy killed in Bulletface tour bus shooting Thursday night; no suspects in custody… "The Versace Mansion," owned by*

American billionaire Alexus Costilla, 31 wounded in gun violence across Chicago since Thursday; Bulls player Joakin Noah makes public call for peace… FBI sweeping Chicago for wanted Mexican terrorist Jennifer Costilla; reward to $50 million overnight… Jennifer Costilla is suspected of killing 12 FBI agents and 9 CPD officers in Chicago car bombing… Jennifer Costilla is also suspected of beheading five in string of Chicago murders…

On the screen, two MTN News anchors were discussing the shooting at the Versace Mansion.

"We definitely need to fall off the radar for a while," Alexus said. She bit a chunk out of a hash brown and shoveled in some grits and omelet behind it. She chewed and swallowed and drank some milk. "I've been considering buying an island like the one Mariah and Nick bought. That way, we can go and be alone whenever we want to get away from it all."

"Sounds like the best idea to me."

"We'll be like Beyoncé and Jay-Z."

"Don't start that shit again."

"Start what?"

"Comparin' us to them. We're in our own lane."

"We're the highest-paid couple; they're the second highest-paid couple. Same category, ain't it?" She turned and smiled at him. "I suppose you're right, though. I mean, who can compare to Bulletface?"

"Nobody. Ever."

She finished breakfast and set the tray on her nightstand. Getting out of bed, she caught Blake biting down on his bottom lip and ogling her rotund backside as she sauntered off to the bedroom in her white-lace Victoria's Secret bra and panties set. She brushed her teeth hurriedly and freshened up, anxious to get what she was certain Blake had in store for her.

When she returned to bed moments later, she wasn't at all surprised to find him lying back with his big black love stick in hand. He was wagging it proudly, his diamond encrusted platinum teeth partially exposed in a virile grin.

Her pussy tingled and constricted. She crawled to him, and mounted him. His strong veiny black hands rubbed her ass. She pecked her lips against his.

"Think you can fuck me and only me for the rest of your life?" she asked.

"*Hell* yeah." He lifted his head and got another swift peck. "You're my wife. I don't want nobody else."

"Mmm hmm. You think you're slick, Blake."

"How do I think I'm slick?"

"That breakfast in bed. You only brought it to warm me up so you can get your little dick wet."

"No I didn't"

"There's a reason for everything."

"And ain't shit little about Monster."

"I've seen bigger," she lied, smiling.

Blake clamped his hands on her waist and rolled so that he was on top of her. He said, "Don't get fucked up," then his face disappeared between her thick thighs.

She felt the warmth of his breath through the fabric of her panties. He moved them aside with a curled fingertip and buried his tongue deep between the lubricious fold of her pussy. He licked her there for at least a full minute before pushing up her abundantly meaty legs, peeling off her panties, and going to work on her clitoris, sucking and licking and roughly massaging it with his fingers.

Within seconds, Alexus was gasping erratically. She took off her bra and mashed her breasts together.

"Shit… Fuck… mmm," she moaned, winding her hips.

Blake's lips were locked on her clitoris, and he was swishing saliva around it, flicking his tongue across it. Starry-eyed, she gazed fixedly at his handsome dark face. The sparkle of his teeth paled in comparison to the bling of the diamonds in his necklace and watch. His hairline was perfectly lined. His cologne was a love potion, wafting up her nose and stimulating her senses more than any scent could. She wanted him to stop and allow her the opportunity to please him just as much as he was pleasing her, but his nimble tongue had her on cloud nine.

Moments later she moaned and trembled in orgasm. Blake moved back on his knees and watched her juices escape. His twelve-inch dich was pole-hard, jutting out over his silk Versace boxers; a globule of pre-cum dangled from its bulbous head.

"Yeah," he said, "I'm can definitely fuck you forever."

"Hold on a second," Alexus said breathlessly as she got up and crossed the room to the bureau. She opened a drawer and took out a bottle of baby oil. She handed the bottle to Blake and climbed back onto the bed on her hands and knees.

Blake needed no instructions. He stepped back and removed his jeans with one hand while pouring oil on Alexus' pillowy butt cheeks with the other. He rubbed in the slippery liquid. She bounced her ass, and it jiggled wonderfully.

"Damn, baby. Do that again," he said.

"Do what, this?" She wiggled her thighs. Her ass quaked wildly. "You like that? I learned that from Chyna last night."

He pulled her to the edge of the bed. She was still bouncing her derriere as he stood behind her and guided the crown of his long dick into her wet, hungry, constricting pussy. She pushed back against him, steadily rocking her hips until she was fully impaled, then eased forward and repeated the salacious movements until a rhythmic pounding was established.

His thrusts were ruthless.

Alexus loved every savage penetration. She moaned incessantly. The sunlight beaming in through the open Louis Vuitton curtains was warm on her back. Looking over her shoulder at the herculean musculature of Blake's chest and abdomen, Alexus gasped as she succumbed to a second breathtaking orgasm that sent her body into yet another spell of convulsions.

He held her by the waist and pounded harder.

Suddenly, she scrambled away to safety at the head of the bed. She let out a breathless laugh and signaled for a time-out.

"Fuck you think you're goin'?" He showed an amused smile. "Get back over here. I ain't gon' hurt you."

"Liar. You're trying to kill me."

His smile broadened.

"It's not funny. We're gonna have to find a way to shrink that thing," she said.

"Yeah right."

"I'm not kidding. It's so big it hurts."

"Get over here. I like that position," he persisted, stroking the big black muscle.

She rubbed her stomach worriedly. "You're busting up my insides, rearranging my organs. Think I might need medical attention."

"You gon' need medical attention"—he crawled to her—"if you don't give *me* some attention"—he kissed her lips—"right muhfuckin' now."

She laughed and shoved him onto his back. Mounted him reverse cowgirl style and sucked in a deep breath as he forced her down until nearly his entire length was crammed inside her.

Arching her back and biting her lower lip, she began bouncing up and down. She moved slowly at first, but then the dick started feeling too good and she became a lot more aggressive, slamming herself down on him with reckless abandon. She looked back and saw that he was clearly enjoying the ride; his teeth were clenched, and his expression was tight.

"That's what I'm talkin' bout, baby. Break this dick," he said.

"You want me to break it?"

"Mmm hmm. Break this muhfucka."

Alexus bounced harder, cradling her breasts in her hands. Then she turned around to face him and continued the relentless ride. He dug his fingers into the fleshy cheeks of her ass. Seconds later, a third orgasm froze her in place. Blake kept going, thrusting upward and grinning up at her as her juices cascaded down his distended pole.

She collapsed onto his chest. He juggled her ass in his hands, grinding up into him.

"Shit," she said.

"Thought you was gon' break it?"

"Did you pop a Viagra or something?"

"Nah." He kept grinding. "Might be that Lean."

"It's something."

"Hold on… here it… come."

She got up before his semen could spew out and pursed her lips around the head of his dick. Gripping and stroking it in both hands, she sucked on the head until his thick cum was rocketing up into her throat. The heavy load of semen clung to her tongue and the roof of her mouth. She opened up and showed it to Blake, then swallowed just in time to catch the string of cum that was sliding down the side of his twitching erection. She slurped it up, sucked the last few drops out of him, kissed the head good-bye, and flung herself onto the pillow next to Blake's. He grinned at her.

"I can't stand your black ass," she said.

"What I do?"

"You just tried to kill me with that thing."

"I tried to love you wit' it."

"My legs won't stop shaking."

"That's a good thing, ain't it?"

"Yeah, but I still can't stand you. Hand me my panties."

"What's the magic word?"

"Or else," she said, and punched his chest.

Chapter 39

Enrique was sitting in a ladder-back chair in the hall when Blake followed Alexus out of the bedroom. She'd put on a white Chanel jumpsuit and heels, and she was glowing.

"That was—well, it *sounded* amazing," Enrique said as he got up and preceded them to the elevator.

Alexus blushed and looked down at her smartphone.

Blake chuckled, and received another punch for the transgression.

In the elevator, Blake phoned his brother and his music manger to cancel all of his upcoming shows and appearances. They weren't happy about it, but they understood. At a time like this, he had to be home with his family.

"You didn't have to do that," Alexus said, resting her cheek on his shoulder.

"Gettin' myself ready to be a husband."

"You're ready. Don't stress yourself over it. I've already talked to a wedding planner. And Vera Wang will be here at noon tomorrow to take my measurements. I want diamonds all over my dresses. White diamonds. She said they'll probably cost anywhere between two and three million apiece."

"Dresses? How many dresses you need to get married?"

"Just four: one to wear to the venue, one for the actual ceremony, one for the celebration afterward, and one to leave in. See. Four."

Blake shook his head. "Crazy."

The elevator doors parted, and the three of them headed to the spacious all-white living room where they found their children and Tamera sitting on a large blanket in front of the fireplace. They were playing Monopoly on a custom-made golden board. The cash in their hands was real.

Mercedes and Porsche were curled up on the sofa with their phones in their hands. Porsche's face lit up when she saw Blake. He was her favorite rap star.

"Daddy, look!" King shouted, holding up his Monopoly fortune. "I won all these moneys, and Vari barely got *any* moneys."

"Shut *up*." Vari rolled her eyes.

Alexus gave Mercedes a sympathetic hug. Then she and Blake went to the vacant sofa and sat down. Enrique stood behind them.

"That FBI agent was here last night," Alexus said to Blake. "Can you believe that motherfucker had the nerve to ask me for a loan? He asked for forty grand."

"Fuck that pig."

"I'm giving it to him. Who knows, we might need him one day. He'll owe us."

"I wouldn't piss on him if he was on fire."

"We might need him. Forty grand isn't much to pay for an FBI favor."

"Lucky I wasn't here."

"You can't be gangster all the time."

"I'm just bein' me." Blake was Googling, *Bulletface* on his smartphone to see the latest internet gossip, and indeed there was new gossip.

By the time he noticed Alexus had her eyes on his phone, it was too late.

BulletFace seen leaving NYC concert with Tahiry; social media-TMZ.com

Have BulletFace and Alexus called it quits?
Controversial concert video sparks
speculation-Bossip.com

"You must wanna get slapped." Alexus got angry fast. "On my father's grave if you did *any*thing with her, you and I are going have some serious problems."

"I didn't fuck that girl."

"What *did* you do?"

"Nothin'. She came wit' me to the airport after they shot up my car."

"What was she doing with you in the first place?" Alexus snapped.

"Baby. Chill out a li—"

"Don't 'baby' me. Tell me. What was she doing with you? I really wanna know. Tell me."

"Stop trippin'. I told you. It was nuthin'."

"Should I cancel our wedding plans? Let me know now. Don't have me walking down the aisle, dedicating my life to you, if you're not ready."

Porsche butted in: "Girl, please. How you gon' cuss him out about Tahiry when you had Trey

Songz rubbin' all on yo' feet, carryin' you to bed—the whole nine."

Blake furrowed his brows at the back of Alexus' head; she was glowering at the whistle-blower.

"Don't mean-mug me for bustin' you out," Porsche said, "Shouldn't throw stones if you live in a glass house."

When Alexus turned back to Blake, she had a guilty smile on her face. She patted his knee.

"Nuh uh." He shook his head. "Fuck is up wit' that shit? You had Trey Songz in our bedroom?"

"Rubbed her feet, too," Porsche said.

"Shut up, Porsche," Alexus retorted. She was still smiling at Blake. Now, instead of patting his knee, she was rubbing it. "I love you, boy. You know that. Love you with all my heart."

"Yeah, a'ight." The threat behind Blake's tone was evident.

"You'll make a great husband."

"You'll make a great domestic violence victim," he threatened.

"You wouldn't hit me."

"Stop playin' wit' me, Alexus."

She outstretched her legs on the sofa, laid her head on his lap, and looked up at him. "We didn't do anything. I hurt my ankle; he massaged it."

"I'ma hurt yo' ass."

"I might like that."

For a moment, Blake grinded his teeth together and regarded Alexus with an icy stare. The thought of Alexus making love to another man infuriated him.

He relaxed his livid expression abruptly and replaced it with a vengeful smile.

I got Tahiry's number, he thought.

"What are you thinking?" Alexus asked.

"Nothin'."

"I don't like that smile."

The vindictive smile burgeoned.

"I'm not letting you out of my sight from here on out," Alexus said.

Blake chuckled and glanced over at the long pair of chocolate legs extending from Porsche's extremely short denim shorts to her baby blue open-toe heels. Her halter was plain white. The bra behind it matched her heels and the paint on her fingernails. Two cushions down from her, Mercedes sat wearing a short black dress and red-bottomed black heels.

Mercedes had tears in her eyes.

"Look at your sister," Blake said.

Alexus didn't look. She whispered, "I know. I saw. There's nothing I can do to comfort her. I wish there was, but there's nothing that can replace the loss of your children."

"Killin' Jenny might help."

"Yeah, but nobody can find her," Alexus said just as her phone began vibrating in her white croc-skin Birkin bag. She took it out and answered.

Alexus' perfect face had a thin veil of makeup. Seconds after she put the smartphone to her ear, the reddish-brown color remained but the blood drained out of the skin beneath it. Her eyes widened.

"What?" Blake asked, instantly worried. There was never any telling what kind of deadly situation awaited with the Costillas.

"It's my… Uncle Flako." She handed the phone to Blake.

"What it is, Flako?"

"I just got word that a thousand Zetas have entered California through a drug tunnel in Tijuana, Mexico. They came in with hundreds of assault rifles, shoulder-mounted rocket launchers, machetes, handguns, and a variety of bomb-making materials. Gamuza sent them, but Jen's financing the operation. They're coming after you and Alexus."

"You think they're here in Miami," Blake asked.

"That's where they were headed four hours ago. They're all in cars and trucks, split up into different groups. You've got some time. But if I were you, I'd be on a plane as soon as possible. The Mexican equivalent of al-Qaeda is headed your way, and they're not coming to talk."

Chapter 40

'...Pull up to ya party, bitch, I got my .40
Pull up to ya house, ay, all dem guns is out, ay
Pull up on ya block, ay, we love pullin' up
And we pullin' up wit Glocks, ay, we all toolied up

We watchin' out for cops, we watch' out for opps
And we watchin' out for thots, cause they be pullin'
up
Watchin' out for paparazzi, they be quick to put cha
up
I pull up I got my Glock and I am quick to pull it up
Ay, ay... Fuck poppin' out, we poppin' up
Ay, ay... We poppin' up, up out the cut, ay
Shooters on the roof, on top o' da cut, mane
I'm movin' overseas, I'm tired o' da drug game
Cause it got dem coppers pullin' up
Dey knockin' and I'm what dey lookin' fuh
I just have my partnas pullin' up
I just heard the opps is pullin' up
We ready to fire dem pussies up
We been in a lotta bullet wars
And we done bought a lotta bullets for em...'

There were over a hundred Black Disciple gang members standing out on 63rd and Eggleston. Most of them were teenagers with dreadlocks dangling over their faces. Every one of them toted pistols and submachine guns equipped with extended clips. They were sipping Lean, smoking the best Kush in Chicago, drinking Remy and Hennessey, and popping Molly and Ecstacy pills, while laughing and flirting with the dozens of scantily-dressed black girls who'd come out to party with Englewood's most infamous gang of killers.

The gang's chief was an eighteen-year-old rap star and one of the most ruthless gunslingers Chicago had ever birthed. His name was Chief Keef, and he was sitting on the hood of his black BMW X6, nodding his head to "Pull Up" as it bumped out of the SUV's speakers.

He passed a blunt to Tadoe, his cousin and fellow GBE rapper.

Tadoe was distraught, but he was hardly showing it. Last night his brother Lil Dave had been shot dead at the Citgo on 116th and Michigan.

"Folks, that nigga Bulletface gotta get it," Tadoe said.

"On David," Chief Keef agreed. "Fuck-nigga lucky we wasn't there."

"Tray Savage was chasin' some goofy ass thot, got lil bruh bodied."

"We all done did it before. Cain't blame Tray Savage."

"He say that thot who set him up dance at that strip club out west."

"Which strip club?" Keef asked, taking a sip of Lean.

"The one on 16th and Homan."

"You mean 16th and Trumbull?"

"Yeah, that one."

"Redbone's."

Tadoe nodded and coughed a couple of times. "Yep. On David. That's where we met them Sicko Mob niggas at, remember? The lil niggas who made that "Maserati" song wit' Durk."

"Cup the chief of the Travelers over there."

"On David, he is."

"Think that's where Bulletface be at a lot. Alexus got a big ass house on Trumbull. Bulletface and Cup be together a lot. And I think Bulletface still got that mansion he bought from MJ in Highland Park."

"We gon' catch that fuck-nigga in traffic." Tadoe passed Keef the blunt and took a sip of his own Lean, which he'd mixed with a bit of Molly. "We can find that stripper bitch who set up Tray

Savage. Her name is Bubbles. Bitch go a big stupid ass booty, on David. You gotta remember her. She had on the red thong that night we went to Redbone's."

"How the fuck I'm s'posed to remember that shit?"

"*I* remember."

"Bitch, you don't remember that shit." Keef threw a sharp jab that connected with Tadoe's left jaw. Then he jumped off of the BMW, laughing.

Tadoe's face turned serious; he didn't find it funny.

Several BD's joined in on the laughter.

"Folks," Tadoe said, "on BDN, I'll beat yo' ass."

The laughter went on for close to a minute.

Then it stopped suddenly as a thuggishly-dressed teenager came walking around the corner with an older man who looked to be his father. The teen's hat was cocked to the right. The words BRICK SQUAD were written across the chest of his black t-shirt in big blue letters, and beneath them were the numbers 069.

Brick Squad was a crew of Gangster Disciples originating from 69th and St. Lawrence.

Chief Keef and his O-Block BDs were at war with Brick Squad, had been for years.

The girls moved out of the way as all eyes fell on the Brick Squad affiliate.

"Oooh shit," said a thot. "That's Marley from Brick Squad, Jah-Jah's nephew."

Chief Keef smiled. "Let me get this one," he said, pulling the .40-caliber Glock from his hip and running toward the unsuspecting victim.

Marley was looking down at his smartphone. By the time he looked up, Chief Keef was no more than twenty feet away from him on the sidewalk. He grabbed the older man's arm and tried to turn and flee.

Aiming carefully, Chief Keef pulled the trigger repeatedly.

BANG! BANG! BANG! BANG! BANG! BANG! BANG! BANG! BANG! BANG!

Both Marley and the older guy who looked like him took multiple bullets to their heads, necks, and chests. They died instantly.

"Fuck-niggas," Keef said as he ran back to his BMW.

He handed the gun off to one of the guys and jumped in the driver's seat. Tadoe got in next to him. Fredo Santana and Ballout got in the backseat and Keef sped off, along with twenty other cars full of Black Disciples.

"We gon' catch Bulletface the same way," he said.

"On David," Tadoe said.

Chief Keef upped the volume on his *Bang 3* album, checked the rearview mirror, and then relaxed, leaned back in his seat, and drove.

'...You gon' smell the coffee, come through chalkin', ay
Have this pistol on me, come through sparkin', ay
Have my dogs wit' me, come through barkin', ay
You ain't have no fuckin' business talkin'...'

Chapter 41

Looking down at Thunder, T-Walk balled his fist into her hair and forced his dick to the back of her throat.

She gagged. Her eyes watered. A furry pair of handcuffs restrained her hands behind her back. She was on her knees in T-Walk's private office at The Swagger, The nightclub he owned in Michigan City, Indiana. Lately, she'd been reading *Fifty Shades of Grey* on her Kindle tablet and T-Walk guessed that had something to do with her new handcuffs fetish.

It was 10:00 A.M. Central Standard Time, according to his rose-gold Rolex timepiece. He was dapper in a light blue Hugo Boss suit and tie. His pants and boxer-briefs were in a pool around his ankles, and his eyes were on his beautiful Nigerian fiancée.

He dug in her throat until she pulled back, coughing and gasping for air. Then she began sucking him tightly, in and out of her throat. She was nude, except for the Zanotti pumps on her pretty pedicured feet. Her white Gucci dress lay in a heap next to T-Walk's glass desk.

One wall consisted of darkly tinted glass, overlooking the club's expansive blue marble floor below, where over three hundred high-ranking Gangster Disciples from all over the country stood in wait of T-Walk's arrival. The navy blue Gucci suits they all wore had been purchased by T-Walk, though the crew of drug-dealers and robbers they ruled over kept them well above the poverty line. They were eating from plates of steak and lobster, also provided by T-Walk.

His Samsung Galaxy S5 rang on the desk. Cup's contact picture—a photo of Cup and his partner Lil Cholly standing beside a black Lamborghini Gallardo on 15th and Trumbull—appeared on the screen. T-Walk stepped back to pick it up; Ashley's steadily slurping mouth moved with his erection.

"What it look like, Cup?"

"Nigga, you know what the fuck it look like. You sent them niggas to shoot up *my* block last night. They shot my *son*, nigga. They shot Bankroll Rece. We atcho ass, nigga. Let a muhfucka catch you back in Chiraq, nigga. It's gunplay on—"

"Fuck you niggas, I'm war ready. Let me see you go to war against ten thousand guns. You wanna play? We can play in every mothafuckin' city we catch you niggas in!"

"That's the thought," Cup said and ended the call abruptly.

T-Walk wasn't done ranting.

"He want war, too! Nigga, we all can go to war! I got seventy million in dirty money to blow on guns! Five grand'll get a fuck-nigga wacked!"

Ashley slipped her mouth off of his saliva-coated phallus and looked up at him.

He said, "They're dead, baby. Bulletface is dead. Cup is dead. Their families are dead. The bosses are standing downstairs wait for me to give the word. And guess what, I'm about to push that mothafuckin' button."

"Do you want me to finish or not?" Ashley asked. "I'll get up and leave you alone with your feelings if you—"

"No, no, no," he said quickly. His truculent scowl turned into a smile. "Go ahead, baby. Do your thing."

Ashley giggled and continued sucking him.

Leaning back on the desk, Trintino Walkson ruminated over the war that was inches from spilling into the streets all across America.

He was ready for it.

Chapter 42

"You see, son, they have a name for people like Alexus. She's a celebrity and that's just something a cartel boss can't be. So what she was groomed by Papi; that doesn't make her worthy of bossing us around. We're here in Mexico doing all the dirty work while she's running around showing off her big butt like a damned Kardashian."

Pedro Costilla nodded in agreement, but he didn't really agree with his father. He hardly ever agreed with his father. Flako Costilla was a Mexican Tyrant, directly responsible for thousands of murders all across Mexico, Guatemala, Honduras, Nicaragua, Costa Rica, Panama, and even in the South American countries of Colombia, Peru, and Bolivia. He'd beheaded hundreds of men and women for the most frivolous of reasons.

The two of them were in the backseat of Flako's pearly white armored Suburban with gold-plated AK-47s on their laps. There were seventeen more armored SUVs full of Costilla Cartel militants speeding up the dusty Ciudad Juarez road. The pickup trucks leading and trailing them had .50 caliber machine guns attached to their roofs, and they were manned by the cartel's best gunners.

"So," Pedro asked, "How is this plan of yours going to work? What if Alexus doesn't go to Chicago?"

"She'll go. Mercedes has to bury her little ones."

"This is a bad idea."

"How so?"

"Jenny's gonna kill Alexus."

"What's so bad about that?"

"We've buried way too many Costillas. Alexus is a good kid. She's never done anything to deserve all the shit she's going through. I mean, it's not like she *asked* to inherit this thing of ours. Granny Costilla left it to her, and her life's been nothing but hell ever since."

"Save me the tears, will you?" A heartless chuckle rumbled out of Flako's throat. "With Alexus out of the way, this cartel will belong to me."

"But it already belongs to you. It's the *Costilla* cartel; it belongs to all of us."

"You going soft on me?"

"I just don't want to see another Costilla in the grave, and that's where you're leading Alexus. Besides, why work with Aunt Jenny after seeing what she did to Antoney? She recorded herself cutting off your son's head and put it online for all the world to see."

"Yeah, and Alexus murdered your sister."

"Bella deserved it. She had Blake's parents killed. We didn't approve that hit. But none of that has anything to do with you helping Aunt Jenny take out Alexus. I know what you're up to, father. This meeting says it all"

"You're smarter than you look," Flako said, slapping a mammoth paw atop Pedro's head and shaking it fiercely.

They arrived at a small diner that stood between two boarded up shops on a narrow road in northern Juarez. Several teams of opposing cartel militants crowded the street.

Flako's men went into the diner to make sure it was safe. Then Flako and Pedro got out and headed inside.

The diner was dark, almost unbearably hot, and heavily redolent of tobacco smoke. Seated around the table at the back wall were three of

Mexico's most feared drug cartel leaders: Carlos Fuentes, boss of the Gulf Cartel; Diego Kahlo, boss of the Sinaloa Cartel: and ninety-something-year-old Gamuza, boss of Los Zeta Cartel. Like Flako and Pedro, they all donned white Hartmarx suits and gold Rolex watches.

"You're late," Gamuza muttered as Flako made it to the table and sat across from him.

"My apologies, gentlemen." Flako gave Gamuza a brief, gelid stare before turning to acknowledge the other two. When Flako was a kid, he'd watched Gamuza take off his father's head with a chainsaw in a bold attempt to seize power of the Mexican drug trade. The macabre memory of Segovia Costilla's brutal murder still lived with Flako.

It was a memory that would never die.

For now, though, it would have to be laid aside in order to make room for what was undoubtedly the biggest power move in criminal history.

The four drug cartels were about to become one, all working beneath the wealthiest cartel boss in history. The four perilous men would be under-bosses.

Alexus Costilla would be the boss of all bosses… at least until Flako got her out of the way.

Chapter 43

"I don't trust Flako," Enrique said thoughtfully.

Alexus had gotten the warning from Flako over an hour ago, and now she and the family were thirty thousand feet in the air in the G6 private jet, soaring over northern Georgia.

She was sitting across Blake's lap in the sumptuous white leather seat across the table from Enrique. The thumbnail of her left hand rested tightly between her teeth. Alexus had phoned in Dr. Melonie Farr before boarding the jet. Now the former "relationship therapist" was across the aisle, offering some kind words to Mercedes and Porsche. Tamera was entertaining the kids in the seats behind Blake's.

"I'll never trust another Costilla for as long as I live," Alexus said," not Flako, not Pedro, and certainly not Jenny. Mercedes and my son are it." She paused and looked at Mercedes. "And I half-way don't trust her ass," she added.

"There's something funny going on with Flako," Enrique said.

"Funny like what?"

"I'm not sure, Alexus. Maybe it's because he hasn't come around since you and Blake had that final talk with Bella. Since then, he's only called to get your approval on drug and cash shipments.

"I was thinking that."

"It's also kind of odd that I didn't get an answer from our men in Chicago when I called before we took off."

"Our men at the Highland Park mansion?"

Enrique nodded his head yes.

"You think something's up?" Alexus asked, her teeth tightening on the thumbnail.

"We'll counter if there's an attack. You can trust me to keep us all safe. I kept your grandmother alive through hundreds of attempts on her life, and that was in Mexico. Safety here in this country is a walk in the park. We can detour and land somewhere else if you'd like, but I don't believe there's a need to. We have more soldiers than Los Zetas could ever dream of having. If they're dumb enough to let Jenny *or* Flako send them on a death march, they deserve every bullet they take to the grave with them."

Alexus displayed a grateful smile. "I thank God for you every day, you know that? You're like an army general."

I am an army general," Enrique grinned, "for the queen of the Americas."

"Flako better not cross me."

"He'll die if he does. All of our men are trained to kill anyone who even remotely threatens the top boss of this cartel. He might go spouting off in English since the vast majority of our men won't understand the language, or maybe to Pedro, but it'll go no further than that."

Alexus went silent. The gentle caress of Blake's hand on her thigh was soothing. She turned to him and saw that he was gazing vacantly out of the window to the right of him, his inquisitive brown eyes lost in the endless sky.

"Think we should turn back," she asked him.

Blake took a moment to ponder his answer before voicing it. "Nah, we're good. We can land at O'Hare," he finally said.

"We don't have to."

"I know."

"We can refuel and keep it moving and rent a suite somewhere in Kansas. Or we can fly to one of our California homes."

"Nah, we'll just get straight on the highway and drive to the Michigan City mansion, stay there until after the funerals, and then we'll all get the fuck away from here for a while. Vacation in Spain or somethin'."

"Ibiza's a nice getaway in Spain. I've been there a couple of times with Papi. You'll like it."

"I wish there was some way we could find that crazy ass aunt of yours."

"You and me both," Alexus replied.

"Papi should've killed that bitch a long time ago."

"I wish he had. She has to be on her way to California if she expects me to meet her in Malibu tomorrow."

"At the yacht, right?"

Alexus nodded. "Yeah, the big boat I'm on in that framed picture on the dining room wall at the Highland Park mansion."

Blake suddenly flicked his eyes to hers.

"Holy shit," Enrique said.

"What?" Alexus asked.

"The picture," Blake said, "the yacht."

Enrique threw himself to his feet. "She said meet her at the Omnipotent! The yacht! Who all knows about that pic—"

"Flako sent me that picture last year."

"Well," Blake said, "there you go. That's gotta be why nobody answered at the Highland Park mansion."

"Absolutely," Enrique agreed. The message she gave Mercedes was more like a riddle. She's counting on you to figure it out, probably thought you'd realize it when she didn't show up at the actual boat in Malibu."

"But how would she know about the picture?" Alexus stood up and looked from Blake to Enrique, planting her hands on her hips. "You think it was Flako?"

"I wouldn't put it past him," Enrique said.

"Are we still over Georgia? Tell the pilot to land in Atlanta. I want every dealer and gangster we supply in the Chicago area to drive out to that

Highland Park mansion with every gun they can get their hands on and shoot any Mexican woman they see. Aunt Jenny can't look too much like her old self if she's traveling around Chicago after killing those cops and FBI agents. I'm guessing she's had some kind of surgery, maybe a lot of it. We might be better off searching for that young guy she was always with."

"We have our own men in Chicago to send to the mansion, eight hundred of them. If she's there, she's dead meat," Enrique said. He went to the cockpit to speak with the pilots.

Alexus mounted Blake's lap facing him. As usual, his hands moved to her derriere and gave it an affectionate squeeze. A mixture of worry and deep thought contorted her pretty face as she locked eyes with him.

"I'm calling Pedro to see what Uncle Flako's been up to lately, as soon as we land. Pedro's always taken a liking to me. He'll tell me everything."

"Don't look so worried, baby," Blake said.

"I'm not worried."

The side of his face drew back in disbelief.

"I'm not," she insisted. "I'm just a little pissed off, that's all. All I want is a peaceful existence, but the underworld is a breeding ground for war and we're trapped smack dab in the middle of it."

"We're good." He kissed her chin, and then her juicy lips. "We ain't got no worries, baby. We can go to the other side of the world and send in the shooters. My Dub Life niggas strapped up. My Travs in Chiraq strapped up. My Lords in Gary got too many choppas. My niggas in the rap game got shooters in their cities. And you got your people, too. Shit, we can go to war. I'm ready."

Chapter 44

The headless bodies of eight bodyguards, two male maids, and a female butler were lying in dried puddles of blood on the white marble foyer floor at the old Jordan mansion in Highland Park. Cyanosis had already taken place. The skin on the decapitated corpses was blue and waxy-looking, almost translucent. The stench of the human waste they had excreted in their underwear upon death combined with the horrendous odor of death itself to create the most putrid smell imaginable.

Jenny Costilla found a bottle of Febreeze and deployed Miguel to the foyer to spray the dead bodies while she relaxed in the chair at the head of the dining room table with a crystal stem-glass full of Ace of Spades champagne. The heads belonging to the reeking corpses sat in plates on both sides of the table. All of them were facing Jenny; their dead eyes were open and she believed they were looking into her soul.

"Don't know what your eyes are searching for," she said to a bodyguard's blue-lipped face. There's nothing but fire inside of this old lady… Good ol' Costilla fire. The good kind of fire, you know? Like a good hell." She dropped her head back and cackled maniacally. "A good hell is a hell of a place to be, am I right? Amazing views.

Beautiful, rolling lawns of flames. Fiery mansions full of cock-suckers like you people. It's the place to be!"

Miguel returned to the dining room wearing a questioning frown.

"Stop talking to the heads," he said.

"They're looking into my soul, Miguel. They're soul-searching."

"You're crazy."

"I most certainly am." Jenny smiled at Miguel. "Our men—are they ready for what's coming?"

"We're prepared."

"I hope Flako's plan to get Alexus here works."

"It might. Mercedes has to come home. Alexus will be somewhere nearby. We'll get her, even if we have to go and find her ourselves."

"We'll rip off her pretty little head," Jenny said. "Bring the Costilla cartel back to its full-blooded Mexican roots. My father will be proud of me. He'll look down on me from—no, he'll look *up* at me, from the good hell."

"The good hell?"

"Yes. The good hell."

"You're good and crazy."

"Indeed I am."

Jenny drank some more champagne. Shaking his head, Miguel turned to leave... and froze at the booming sound of machine gun fire.

Chapter 45

"Holy shit, she's really there," Enrique said.

"Doesn't look anything at all like Aunt Jenny to me," Alexus said.

"Oh, it's her alright. Look at that walk. That's Jenny's walk. I know that walk from a mile away."

The Gulfstream 650 had landed at Hartsfield-Jackson a couple of minutes ago, and now everyone, except Tamera and the kids, was huddled around Alexus' laptop computer, watching and rewinding and watching again the short surveillance camera footage of a man and a woman approaching the Highland Park mansion in Chicago. The man threw a hook-ended rope over the red brick wall that surrounded the property and used it to quickly climb up the wall. There he waited for the woman, and together they took the leap to the lawn below, where they waited. Seconds later, two black vans pulled up to the wrought-iron front gate. A dozen masked men rushed out of the vans with assault rifles strapped to their backs. A couple of them carried their own grapnel ropes, and soon they were over the wall and running toward the mansion.

Then the video turned into static.

The power had been cut.

"This was yesterday?" Mercedes asked. Her distraught green eyes were hidden behind gold-framed Chanel sunglasses that she had somehow snagged from Alexus' closet.

"Yeah," Enrique said, "and my guess is she's still there. Our men should have arrived by now. They'll be calling me back when the area's secure."

Blake kissed the nape of Alexus' neck and left his lips there for a long moment. He was standing behind her with his arms encircling her slender waist.

"I hope they kill that crazy bitch," Porsche said.

"They'll get her," Alexus said hopefully.

Just then, the jingle of a FaceTime alert rang from Enrique's iPhone5.

All eyes went to the smartphone.

The video popped on.

Alexus and Mercedes gasped.

A blonde-haired woman was sitting on the marble kitchen floor with her back against the blood-splattered stainless steel refrigerator door. There were bullet holes in her black dress, and blood was spilling over her trembling lower lip. Her face was drawn tight in a frigid scowl.

It was Jennifer Costilla. Blake was certain of it. She'd obviously gone through several surgical procedures, but a lot of her distinct features remained.

"Alexus Costilla!" Jenny shouted. "You're no cartel boss! You fucking celebrity! I knew you wouldn't come! You're afraid! El Jefes don't—" she coughed and blood sprayed from her mouth— "fear… they don't…"

"Shoot her in both hands," Alexus said, snatching the phone from Enrique.

Two black-suited men with silenced handguns moved forward, pressed them against Jenny's hands, and pulled the triggers.

Pop! Pop!

Jenny growled in pain.

"Now the kneecaps and the elbows," Alexus said.

"Coward!" Jenny screamed.

Pop! Pop! Pop! Pop!

"Now cut off her fucking head," Alexus said, gritting her teeth.

A bloody smile crossed Jenny's face. "You have no idea what you'll have... on your hands... if you... kill..." Her words trailed off as her throat was sliced open with what looked like a standard butcher knife.

Porsche gasped and turned away.

"Oh, Jesus," Dr. Melonie Farr exclaimed.

No one else said a word as the knife-wielder jammed a knee into Jenny's chest and went to work, sawing through her neck. The decapitation took less than a minute. When it was done, the Costilla Cartel thug held up her dripping head for Alexus to see it.

Blake let go of Alexus as she and Mercedes fell into each other's arms. He looked at Enrique and let a heavy breath escape his nose.

"Finally," Enrique said, pocketing his smartphone. "Maybe now we can have a little peace."

Then Blake's smartphone rang.

Chapter 46

Young Meach was calling.

Blake stepped into the private jet's restroom and took the call.

"Man, where you at, bruh?" Meach asked.

"At the airport in Atlanta. Why? What's up?"

"We just found that Hummer in Gary. It was parked at the Champ's liquor store on 17th and Grant. Bruh, we aired that muhfucka out, 'bout a hun'ed rounds, on Angelo. Me and Scrill. All three o'da niggas in it died, but the nigga Ant got away. He dipped off through da alley. Disappeared on me. Rube caught his brother around the corner and gave him half the fifty out the K. We out here layin' niggas down, bruh. Shootin' hats off while you cakin' wit' the queen."

"Fuck you, bruh," Blake retorted.

Meach laughed. "Just fuckin' wit'choo, bruh. We got this shit out here. You kick back. Be the captain and let the soldiers work. Don't even think about that GD shit Cup just called talkin' 'bout. We gon' handle—"

Blake heard screeching tires through the phone, followed by the thunderous drum of fully-automatic gunfire.

"Shit," he heard Meach whisper. Then came the sound of more screeching tires and the call ended.

Three callbacks yielded no answer.

Just as his thumb was descending for a fourth attempt, Cup called.

Reluctantly, Blake answered. "You called Meach?" he asked immediately.

"Yeah. Was callin' you next. Just lettin' you know that now we're in the same boat."

"Fuck are you talkin' about?"

"You ain't heard?" Cup seemed surprised. "The GDs, the BDs—they all got hits out on you, and they're at me too. We gotta strap up and go to war wit' these niggas. We got to, Lord. After this shit, we can part ways. But for now, we gotta unite to fight off the opps. You're the king of the Midwest, and I'm the king of Chicago. We in this shit together or what?"

Blake pondered his answer while studying his diamond-encrusted platinum teeth in the oval mirror over the sink. The bathroom door opened and Alexus walked in with her hands on her hips. She shut the door, locked it, and leaned back against it, staring at Blake with a beaming smile on her face.

"Nah," he said to Cup. "I already got a partner in crime and we're ready for war. You handle your end, I'll handle mine."

Ending the call, Blake sat the smartphone on the sink and slid the palms of his hands down his face.

"Yes!" Alexus said triumphantly. "We got that bitch. We finally got that bitch." She stepped in front of Blake and pressed her lips to his. "I just got off the phone with Pedro. Enrique's out there talking to him now. You're not going to believe what just happened in Mexico."

"What happened?" His hands found her derriere and squeezed.

"My Uncle Flako made a deal with the other three most powerful drug cartels in Mexico. Now they're all a part of the Costilla Cartel, and I'm the top boss. That gives me power over all of Mexico. Every gram of coke that comes into this country from now on will be from me."

Blake kissed the top of her nose. "That's good. We'll need all the help we can get. The GDs and the BDs got hits on me. Cup just told me."

"So what?" she shrugged and began unfastening his Louis Vuitton belt. "We're more than ready for any war that comes our way."

Epilogue

Rapper Bulletface and corporate business mogul Alexus Costilla tied the knot Friday evening in a private ceremony at their Malibu home… The multibillionaire couple reportedly paid Beyoncé $5 million to sing at the wedding… "Bulletface and Alexus are honeymooning in Ibiza, Spain," says a source close to the couple. "They can't keep their hands off each other."

Alexus finished reading the words that were scrolling across the bottom of CNN and turned off the 50-inch flat screen television on the wall across from their bed. It was 10:15 P.M. in Ibiza.

The ocean-front mansion Blake and Alexus were honeymooning in was three stories tall and worth $65 million. They were renting it from a Saudi prince for $500,000-a-night. To Alexus Costilla-King, it was worth every cent.

Her pussy was sore; Blake had spent the majority of the day abusing it with his twelve-inch python. Now he was lying next to her with one arm outstretched, twirling her hair around his fingertips while she sat Indian-style and gazed down at his sparkling grin.

"How does it feel to be a husband?" she asked, lightly scratching her fingernails across his strong dark chest.

"Best feelin' ever, baby," he said.

"It feels so good to be Mrs. King. I've fought long and hard with your black ass to get this far."

"I got something long and hard you can fight." His grin burgeoned.

"I've already lost that fight."

"You might win round two."

"Round *two*?" she scoffed. "More like round *fifty*-two. Look at my legs. They're still shaking. You can't keep pounding me like you're drilling for oil every time we fuck. That shit hurts."

He grabbed her elbow and pulled her on top of him, kneading her meaty ass in his hands. He had on a pair of white silk Versace boxers and nothing else. Alexus was nude.

The warmth of her pussy on the underside of his dick began to harden it.

He slapped his hands on her ass.

"How's Meach doing?" she asked.

"He a'ight."

"Alright? He got shot twice."

"In the wrist and the chest," Blake said dismissively.

"Don't be so insensitive. Bullet wounds hurt."

"How would you know?"

"I watched you recover from two of them when that psycho bitch Nauti shot you, remember? You didn't just brush that off."

Blake smiled and rubbed her ass.

His dick was growing harder by the second.

"There's something I have to tell you," Alexus said. "Well… actually two things."

"Tell me."

"Okay, the first is that I have to fly to Mexico on the twenty-ninth to meet with the underbosses. We're getting ready to make the smaller cartels an offer to join forces with us."

"What's the offer?"

"Silver or lead."

"Bully."

"Enrique suggested it. Don't blame me. He told me to show up and throw my weight around a little; a show of power, you know. Let them know who's boss. I'll only be there for a few days, just to show my face. I'll be back in time for your first show."

Blake's music manager had already taken advantage of the hype surrounding the newlyweds, booking a sixteen-city North American tour—aptly named the "Took the Throne" tour—that would add an estimated $85 million to Blake's net worth.

"The second thing is… I missed my period," Alexus continued.

"You pregnant?"

"I might be. I bought a home pregnancy test. It's in my bag."

In a quick roll, he clamped his hands on her hips and she wrapped her legs around his muscle-laden waist as he stood and walked to the bureau where her white croc-skin Chanel bag sat. She picked up the bag, sucking his upper lip into her mouth.

His phallus was as hard as a flagpole between her thighs as he carried her into the bathroom.

Instead of letting go of her in front of the gold-plated toilet as he'd intended, he pressed her back to the wall and thumbed down his boxers. Holding the base of his perilous pole in his right hand, he prodded the head into her juicy nookie and then jammed it in to the hilt.

She gasped deeply as her angelic green eyes rolled up in their sockets.

"What we gon' name him?" he asked.

Then he began pounding in and out of her.

The End...

Keep reading for acknowledgements and a sneak peek of Bulletface 3…

Acknowledgements

My heart is with my biggest supporters:

Prentice	Harrison
Cassandra	Sarah
Kenneth	George, Sr.
Tanisha	Chanel
Bone	Mariah
Sweet	Shakia
Jesse	Lil Rodney
Micki	Bankroll Rece
Georgia	Hove
Hattie	Roz
Yay	Meach
George	Mama Meach
James	Lacresha
Denise	Crystal
Dale	Britney
Harrietta	Ebanee
Shirley	Tasia

Bulletface

Ashley Hunt

OG Jeff Cooper

Boogie Diggs

Dinero Jones

Cece

Shay

Rita

Khalil Amani

Tysheka

Will

Johnesha Reed-
Hodges

Amy Annette
Gillespie Withers

LaVonda Lovinglife

Sade Dobbs

Yara Kaleemah

Bartholomew Edgerin
Piccolo

Priscilla Murray

DeShawn French

Pam Williams

MzNicki Ervin

Tiara Mack

Nikkinew Jackson

Na'jara Ob

Latasha 'shine' Mack

Angela Jackson

Donica NicaBoo
James-Edgerton

Sabrina Victorian

Ayana Knight

Schawanna Morris

Jenell
Gettingbacktohappy
Proctor

Cherrelle Colarusso

Antoinette Mitchell-
Tate

Diamond Maynard

Areya Wrighter-
Square

Bulletface

Michelle Sanford Harvey

Kesa Muhammad

Kevin Earl

Terrineka Earl

Demetria Scott

Aesha Carroll

Jennifer White

Coco J

Nika Michelle

Kierra Petty

Teruka Carey

Shelli Marie

La'Tonya West

Jason Hooper

Huey

Sawbuck

The Whole Sicko Mobb Gang

Dub Life

Melonie Frazier

Angel SouthwestCandylady Harris

Lykisha Harris

Alyssa Mcbride &

MizzLadii Redd

Sneak Peek...

Bulletface 3: War Ready

Prologue

July 31, 2014
Soldier Field
Chicago, IL

"BULL-ET-FACE! BULL-ET-FACE! BULL-ET-FACE!"

Blake was standing on a circular platform that was set on an electronic timer to make a pneumatic rise to the stage above in less than sixty seconds. He wore lose-fitting, black, leather Louis Vuitton sweat pants, a million-dollar necklace full of 12-carat flawless white diamonds, his half-million-dollar white diamond Hublot watch, and white Louboutin sneakers. Ten-carat white diamonds were set in his gold earrings and pinkie rings. A Louis Vuitton bandana hung from the cash-filled left pocket of his sweats. Nothing hung from the cash-filled right pocket.

Alexus and the kids stood to his left and Kenneth Lerone, his music manager, was at his right.

"Shut it down out there, Blakey," Alexus said, patting and rubbing his shoulder. "Over sixty thousand fans waiting on you out there who paid over a hundred dollars apiece to see you tonight. Don't let them down. Do it for the Kings."

Taking a deep breath, Blake tightened his grip on the diamond-encrusted microphone in his hand, clenched his teeth, and kissed his wife's succulent lips.

"I got this, baby," he said. "Just keep the kids close to you. I'll be done with this concert in no time."

"Can we play monopoly when we get home tonight?" Vari asked.

Blake looked down at his eight-year-old daughter and smiled. "Yeah, Vari, we can play monopoly. Take your brother over there and sit down. Keep your brother occupied and I'll get you your own pizza right after the show. Deal?" he asked as he stuck out his hand to shake on it.

Savaria sealed the deal with one hand while balling the collar of King Neal's shirt in the other. "Come on, boy," she said, snatching him along beside her as she dashed toward a row of chairs.

Following another kiss from his wife and a few encouraging words from Kenneth Lerone, Blake stood on the platform and turned into Bulletface.

The beat to Rick Ross' "War Ready" began booming throughout the stadium. Bulletface had remixed it on his *The Bang Bang Theory* mixtape and it was the song he'd chosen to perform first tonight. This was his first day in Chicago since learning of the hit that the Gangster Disciples and Black Disciples had on his head. He wanted to let the people know how he was feeling about the beefs.

War Ready pretty much summed it up.

He closed his eyes for a couple of seconds as the platform rose to the stage above. Then he took two deep breaths and hit the stage flowing.

'Fourteen bullets hit me, nigga, fourteen!
47s in my Bugatti, hop out let it ring
Before dis rap shit, all I did was bang and slang
caine
I tell my hittas make it rain, dey gon' make it rain
I spent a million on my chain, nigga, plain jane
Anotha million on my rangs, nigga blang blang
Fuck what cha heard, we totin' .40s wit dem
thirties, nigga
Put you in the dirt... now you a dirty nigga
War ready... my shooter wanna gain some stripes
War ready... for five grand he'll take ya life
War ready... I got a billion now who wanna fight'

Sudden pandemonium swept through the crowd as Lil Wayne joined Bulletface onstage to perform his featured verse on the remix. More elated screams followed as Rick Ross and Jeezy came out and performed the original version of the song. Bulletface added to the frenzy by throwing thousands of dollars in hundred-dollar bills into the crowd. Then he launched into "By the Corner Store," another track off *The Bang Bang Theory*.

'I'ma bring somethin' new into town, this Ruger'll pound
P-89 hit you wit' a round
But I ain't gotta get stupid and clown
Cause my goons stay doin' it, and doin' it, and doin' it wild
You and ya guy'll catch two Ls, ya bodies catch a few shells
From somethin' in the trunk that stay bangin' like two twelves
Blakey'll hitchoo wit' that four-four, boy
And leave you slumped on the front steps at Joe-Joe's door
Listen, you won't win, every time you got a beef wit' me
Y'all gon' keep on fallin' like Alicia Keys
And I'ma keep brawlin', just the beast in me
If you thinkin' I'm all cake, come get a piece o'me
And I'ma show you, you don speculated wrong

Bulletface

On the corner broad day, the chrome Tec'll spray ya dome
Niggas on the Ave waitin' for me to call and say it's on
Cause when it's on, we suit up to infiltrate ya home... yeah
You niggas say y'all want some drama, y'all don't want it though
Catch me wit' that choppa out there grindin' by the corner sto'
Where? By the corner sto', Where? By the corner sto'
Disrespect me, dey gon' find you wet up by the corner sto'...

Bulletface was on fifty, and the show was just beginning. He had a few more guest appearances coming up. August Alsina. Rihanna. Meek Mill. French Montana, Yo Gotti, and Rich Homie Quan. It would no doubt be an epic night at Soldier Field. He was certain of it.

In the parking lot outside of the stadium, Bulletface's enemies gathered.

CPSIA information can be obtained
at www.ICGtesting.com
Printed in the USA
LVHW081409020421
683318LV00032B/379